THE REAPER
A LADY OF DARKNESS NOVELLA

MELISSA K. ROEHRICH

Also by Melissa K. Roehrich

LADY OF DARKNESS SERIES

Lady of Darkness

Lady of Shadows

Lady of Ashes

Lady of Embers

The Reaper (Novella)

Lady of Starfire

THE LEGACY SERIES

Rain of Shadows and Endings- Coming August 2023

The Reaper

A COUPLE THINGS

Before you dive into Rayner's story, please know that his novella is dark. It is darker than any of the other *Darkness* books have been. Please make sure you check the trigger warnings. If you're okay with that, I hope you love learning how Rayner became the Fire Court Third.

TRIGGER WARNINGS

Your mental health matters. This book contains descriptive violence and references to SA and resulting trauma. For a full list of possible triggers, please visit my website at https://www.melissakroehrich.com under Book Extras.

PLAYLIST

Music is powerful. When I write I have music blasting in my earbuds. I adore when books come with playlists that follow along with the story. You feel everything more. It immerses you more. It brings everything to life. If you find this to be true for you too, here you go! Enjoy!

Spotify Link:

If you don't have Spotify, or you're reading the physical book, the full Playlist can also be found on my website: https://www.melis sakroehrich.com under Book Extras!

Chateau
Solembra
Fiera
Moutains
Fire
Court
Tana River
Aelyndee
To
Avonleya
<---
Windonelle
Edria
Sea
Baylorin
Water
Court
Anahita's
Springs
Southern
Islands

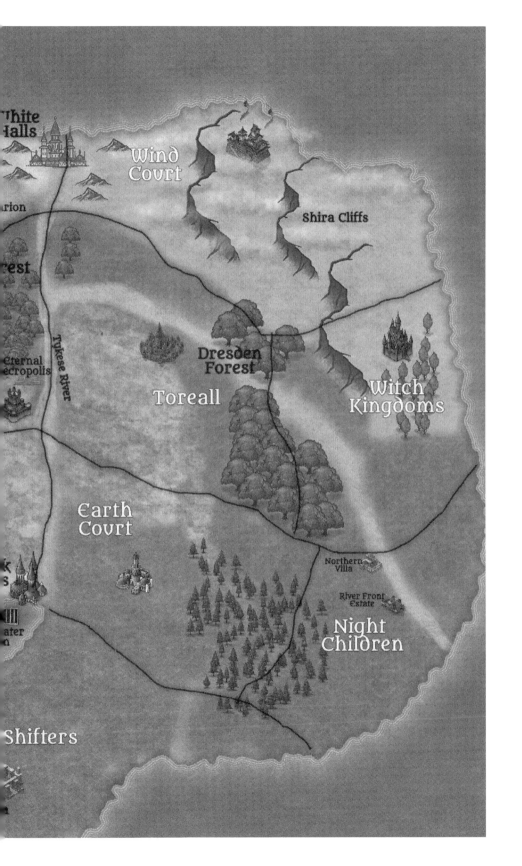

THE ASH RIDER

He waited until Moranna was sleeping. He always did. They had been doing this dance for nearly three years now, ever since he had learned he had sisters.

Two of them.

One full-blooded. One half.

She was pretending she didn't know what he had found out. He was pretending he didn't know she knew.

Rayner slid from the bed. Moranna's naked form didn't move. The white sheet was draped low, exposing her olive skin. Black hair with vibrant red streaks throughout fanned across the pillow. He hadn't been asked to fuck her tonight, but he would have. Anything to keep her focus on him rather than his sisters. She never forced him, as if she were some benevolent master over all of them. As if they were given such a choice.

Wise choices.

That's what she always encouraged them to make.

He'd declined the first few times she'd asked him to come to her bed, finding the idea…awkward to say the least.

He had just been assigned as one of her personal guards after over two decades of training. Two decades of learning to wield ashes as weapons. Two decades of learning to move among the smallest amount of smoke. Two decades of violence and brutality and helping to keep those beneath him in check. It was the natural order of things. He was one of the most powerful Fae on the Southern Islands. Power dictated status. There were few above him, which is why he had been promoted to one of the Baroness's personal guards. He hadn't realized that included serving her in *every* way.

But the first time he'd declined her invitation to her bed, he'd spent the night in a cold sweat. He hadn't slept at all. Anxiety and fear had clawed at him throughout the darkest hours of a day. There wasn't anything in particular that had him pacing around his windowless quarters. He was one of the few Fae who had more than a small bedchamber, but none of the spaces had windows. Not when they were housed inside enchanted cliffs. A colony hidden away from the world for their own protection. If others discovered what kind of power they had, they would want it for themselves. The Baroness kept them protected and safe.

That's what he had been taught to believe.

The second time he had declined her invitation, he'd spent the entire night paranoid that someone had found them. He'd wandered around the various levels of the cliffs like a madman. Not wanting to tell anyone about what was going on and appear weak, he had performed his daily duties without any reprieve the next day.

A few days later, the Baroness had requested he accompany her into one of the producing rooms. He'd never been in one. One of the few rooms he did not have unlimited access to. He'd followed the Baroness up her private endless staircase, her red gown swishing around her ankles. She'd looked back over her shoulder at him, a coy smile he wasn't sure what to do with on her lips, before she held her palm to the door. He'd felt the wards fall, recognizing her touch, and she'd beckoned him to follow her in. When he did, he'd fallen still. There was a young Fae cowering in a corner, tears streaming down her face. She could scarcely be past her first bleeding. She certainly hadn't entered her Staying yet. Her golden hair was a mess, and she was in a nightgown, not the usual white linen shirts and pants everyone wore in the cliffs. Her icy blue eyes were wide and full of terror. A male stood off to the side, arms at his side, wearing only loose-fitting pants.

"I've tried, your Grace," he'd said, his eyes fixed on the ground.

"I know you have, Tyrion," the Baroness had replied sympathetically. "Unfortunately, we need her wind magic, or she would be assigned elsewhere."

The male had said nothing in response, just stood waiting, his eyes never leaving the floor.

The Baroness had moved forward, crouching down before the female. The young Fae had scrambled back, pressing into the corner. "Please, your Grace. Please do not make me do this."

"But you *want* to do this, my dear," she'd coaxed softly, reaching out and brushing back a strand of hair from the girl's face. Her red-painted nail slid along her jaw until she pressed it beneath her chin, tilting her head up. "My sweet child, I need that wind magic to be shared with Tyrion. You desire that too, don't you?"

"I…" She'd faltered, her brow furrowing. She'd shaken her head as if coming out of a trance. "No. I do not want this."

Rayner had watched as the Baroness's lips tipped up into a pleased smile. "You are strong as well. Good," she'd purred. Faster than Rayner could track, the Baroness was gripping the female's jaw, and the girl let out a whimper. He'd forced himself to stay rooted to the spot. "You will do this, Catelyn. And for your insolence, you will not enjoy it, even though Tyrion would have made sure you did. But now you have lost such a privilege. Perhaps next time, you will make wiser choices."

Rayner felt fear and torment and…*lust* ripple in the room. He shouldn't feel any power in this room. The walls were made of shiras-tone to stop Fae from using their power.

Then again, it never stopped him from riding among the ashes.

But the power ripple was not what shocked him. It was that it came from the Baroness. He had always known she was powerful, despite never knowing what her actual gifts were. How else would she maintain control over the hundreds of Fae on these islands? He knew now. The Baroness could manipulate emotions.

She'd stood, staring down at the young female. "But Catelyn?"

"Y-yes, your Grace?" she'd stammered, her gaze fixed on the floor.

"If there is a next time, you will face punishment at the hands of my Ash Rider."

The young female had paled even more, her eyes darting to Rayner, who could only stand there. Just as rumors swirled of the Baroness's power and how you did not wish to be on the receiving end of it, rumors swirled of his own abilities. Some true. Some false. All manipulated by the female who ruled over them.

As Rayner had followed the Baroness out of the room, he'd glimpsed Tyrion moving towards the girl. He'd quickly pulled the door shut behind them. As it clicked into place, the wards reconnecting, the Baroness had turned to face him.

"Will you come to my bed tonight, Rayner?"

He'd known then that she had been the one to torment him for refusing her. He knew if refused again, next time would be even worse. "Of course, your Grace," he'd said gruffly.

She'd reached up, patting his cheek. "It is good to see you making wiser choices."

That was the first time he'd questioned if the Baroness truly desired to keep them safe. He'd never had any reason to believe otherwise until that moment. Why would he? Not when it had been ingrained in him as a youngling that they were only safe because of her. They were blessed by the gods to live away from the rest of the wretched world.

But even on the nights he was not *asked* to fuck her, he slept in her bed. Her "personal guard." That's what she called him anyway. Always by her side.

Her Ash Rider.

He still had his own quarters where his clothing and few personal items were kept, but he only went there to bathe these days. It had only been a year later that he'd discovered he had kin in these cliffs. Then his submission became more about keeping them safe rather than about trying to maintain his own comfort. Ever since that day Moranna had taken him to that producing room, he'd started noticing more and more things. Things that never seemed odd before but now made him uncomfortable. How some younglings seemed to simply disappear. They'd always been told their gifts had emerged and that they'd been assigned to their posts as was custom. But he'd started watching, consciously looking. They were never seen again. Then there were some males and females who looked at the world with dead, vacant eyes. They seemed to see through everyone and rarely spoke. He'd discovered they were all assigned to the producing rooms. He'd dug and dug and learned what happened in those rooms. Eventually he'd learned exactly what the Baroness was trying to do, why they were all here. It was during all this digging he'd come across his own records and learned he had siblings.

Breya and Aravis. Five and seven years of age when he learned of them. Aravis was his full-blooded sister. His mother had apparently died giving birth to her. According to the records, their father had also been a powerful fire Fae. It was his mother that had carried the Ash Rider blood though. There had been other notes written beside his mother's history, but it had been written in a language he could not read. His father had sired Breya with another powerful fire Fae, the female required to drink a tonic of some sort for the duration of her pregnancy. All of this forced in the hopes of his sisters emerging with the Ash Rider gift.

It had taken him two weeks to figure out where they were being held. He'd finally found them in a small room tucked down a side hall on one of the mid-levels. They had been huddled together on a pallet of straw, no fire in the empty hearth. Aravis had black hair like his own and grey eyes. They did not swirl like his did, but his had not started doing that until his gifts had emerged. Breya also had grey eyes, but she had vibrant red hair and freckles smattered across her nose and cheeks. Both girls had shrunk back from him when he'd entered the room.

It took three days before they came near him. It took another few weeks before they began to trust him. Breya was more curious and took to him faster than Aravis did. In time, he'd learned that they were kept in such a dismal state in the hopes that their power would emerge sooner in a bid for survival.

He'd decided then and there he was going to get them out. The simple fact that they had Ash Rider blood meant they were likely destined for the producing rooms. He had often wondered why he had never been sent to one of those rooms yet. It wasn't as if he could ask Moranna. Then she would know what he'd learned.

Moranna.

That was the Baroness's true name. Not that he ever called her that. He had found it written in a letter addressed to her when he'd been searching among her things while she'd bathed one day. The letter had been from someone named Alaric. He'd never learned who that was, but the letter had been written in that same language he had not been taught.

For nearly three years he had bowed to her every whim, had followed orders and carried out her wishes. And for nearly three years, when she slept deeply, he'd slip from her bed. He'd find his sisters, who had been moved to more comfortable accommodations when they had been unable to force their magic to surface. After he'd check on them, he'd disappear among his smoke and ashes beyond the cliff walls and plan how to get them out. He'd visited the main continent, mapped out places they could hide. He'd prepared every last detail all for this night. The night he would take his sisters and leave these godsforsaken islands forever.

Rayner moved silently through the passageways and down the three flights of white stone stairwells to the level where his rooms were located. He'd had small packs ready for weeks so that when the time came, it was one less thing for him to worry about. The packs held a change of clothing for each of them, dried fruit and nuts, small water-skins, and light blankets. Just enough to get them to a location across the island where more supplies were stored. He'd collected funds over the years, enough to pay one of the merchant ships to smuggle the three of them off the islands.

He hadn't told his sisters they were close to being able to leave, not wanting to get their hopes up in case something went wrong and he had to delay things. Their powers still lying dormant was a blessing from the gods, to be honest. The wards around the cliffs picked up magical signatures. They wouldn't have any, and he'd been working his way around them for years. No, the hardest part of this would be getting them out of the cliffs themselves because he could not carry others in his ashes and smoke. They would have to walk out the main entrance that was always monitored by no less than five sentries.

He already knew who was on guard duty tonight. Five sentries who liked to visit the mid-level rooms where the "power vessels" were held. The most powerful Fae who were forced to mate in the hopes of producing even more powerful offspring. "Practice for the producing rooms" the sentries would always chuckle crudely, winking at Rayner on their way by.

He would have no issues sacrificing them tonight. He wouldn't carry guilt for them, unlike some of the other lives he'd been forced to take by Moranna. It didn't matter that he'd had to follow orders to keep others safe, to keep his sisters safe. Those kills still left their marks deep on his soul.

He fished out the packs where he had them stashed into the sleeves of a heavy tunic in the back of his closet. Smoke and ashes swirled around them, taking them to a pocket realm so they wouldn't need to worry about carrying them. He strapped extra daggers to his belt, sliding two more down his boots. A sword was strapped across his back. He swung a cloak around his shoulders, grabbing two smaller ones he'd stashed in the closet as well, before he silently stepped from the room, closing the door softly behind him.

No one would question seeing him in the halls. They wouldn't dare. Not the Baroness's personal guard. No one would say anything as he escorted two younglings throughout the levels. No one would likely bat an eye until he had the girls on the main level, heading for the passageway that would lead out to the beach.

They were older now. Breya was seven, and Aravis was nearly ten, but not nearly old enough to fully understand what was going on. He would get them out, and they could have normal childhoods for what remained of them. Their power could emerge naturally. They would never know hunger or discomfort again. He had shelter secured in the Water Court until he could find a way to obtain a portal to the Fire Court. The girls would both emerge with fire gifts when it came time, so the Fire Court was the obvious choice to make a home. He'd only managed to get to the Fire Court a handful of times in his scouting, but he could already picture their faces when they saw the Twilight Fires on the Tana River for the first time. Breya would giggle in delight. And Aravis? She would smile. A real one. One he had never seen on her face before.

He would tell them of his travels, of the things he had seen beyond the cliff walls. Breya would grow bored rather quickly at her young age. He would let ashes drift through the air for her to chase and play with. But Aravis? She would always ask him to describe the world. The sea. The night sky. Birds and fish and deer. But mostly, she wanted to hear about the sun. About how it gilded the world in light. How it warmed your face. How it rose and set every day, telling the realm when it was day and night.

At dawn, she would see the sun crest the horizon for the first time.

A small smile graced his lips at the thought. He rarely smiled here. Never had a reason to. Perhaps that would change too.

He came to the door of the small room that they had been sharing for the past three months, the wards recognizing his touch as most rooms beneath the cliffs did. He pushed it open, anticipating Breya's excited squeal that came from her every night when he showed up, but what he found made his blood run cold.

Moranna sat cross-legged on one of the small beds. She wore a red gown with deep slits up the side, the dress dipping just as low in the front. Her black hair flowed down around her shoulders, the red streaks glinting in the candles lit throughout the small space.

"Rayner," she said with a pout on her red tinted lips. "I am so disappointed in your poor choices."

"Your Grace," he said, immediately bowing.

The Baroness braced her hands behind her, leaning back on them as her dark eyes surveyed him. "There is no need for pretending, Rayner. Not anymore." He stiffened, standing upright once more. Her lips were curved up in a pointed, malicious smile. "The young ones' gifts emerged today." Her smile morphed into a pout. "So incredibly disappointing. Basic fire gifts. Both of them. One would think with your blood in her veins, the oldest would have at least had a drop of Ash Rider magic. And the younger one? Scarcely magic at all. Mere sparks."

"Where are they?" Rayner demanded, his voice a deadly growl that had Moranna sitting up straighter.

Her eyes narrowed on him. "I would advise you to make wise choices in this moment, Rayner."

"Where are they?" he repeated.

"They have been assigned to their duties, as all Fae in the colony are when they emerge."

"Where are they?" he bellowed, ashes falling from his hands. Hands that were shaking so violently, he couldn't control it.

A faint smile reappeared on Moranna's mouth. "The oldest will be assigned as a power vessel in the hopes that something can still come of that Ash Rider blood. The youngest, however, has been assigned to board the ferries, as she will not be able to contribute anything to the colony."

Rayner was spinning on his heel before the Baroness had finished speaking. He didn't bother with the stairs, moving among the smoke of the sconces that lined the various levels , feeling the grey wisps brush along his being as he went. His boots landed on the stone ground of the main level a minute later, and he was running. There was a door at the back of this chamber. A door he only entered when Moranna required him to end life, usually of those who had committed crimes against the colony. The bodies were loaded onto boats that followed the small stream that ran through the cliffs out to the beach where others were assigned to dispose of them, usually those with fire or earth gifts. But to kill a child? Simply because she would not be power-ful? She could do *something* when she was older. But death?

Icy horror washed through him as realization sank into him. The Fae—the *children*— who would disappear, assigned to duties outside the cliffs. They had all been killed for simply not being powerful enough. For not being born with the gifts the Baroness desired. Who would carry out those types of orders?

But he would have a few years ago. No questions asked if the Baroness had told him it was required to keep them safe. Fuck, maybe he had, and she just hadn't told him the truth about those he had killed. She had never ordered him to kill a child, but would he have questioned her?

He had to believe he would have said no because if not…

But he hadn't said no to any of the orders he'd been given to hand out death. The sword strapped down his back had innocent blood on it. His gifts had been used to maim and destroy and kill those who had never deserved it. Who had simply been born in the wrong place at the wrong moment in time. They had been taught the gods had blessed them to be born away from the world in the safety of the cliffs, when in reality they had been abandoned by the gods and cursed by the Fates.

He skidded to a halt outside the iron door. He couldn't cross the wards to this chamber of his own volition. One of the few rooms he did not have free access to.

Now he knew why.

Two guards came rushing up behind him, confusion etched along their features. "Do either of you have access to this chamber?" Rayner demanded.

"No, Ash Rider," one answered, his confusion shifting to trepidation as he watched Rayner. "Only the Baroness and the Marshals can enter at will."

The Marshals. He'd known they could enter at will, but that was because there were cells in that chamber to hold criminals while they served time for their crimes. Not because…

But the more he thought about it, that fit too. The Marshals not only oversaw the cells, but were in charge of the overseers who monitored the Fae and one Marshal, Feris, was the Captain of them all. He was a mean fucker that Rayner was grateful he'd rarely had to deal with, let alone answer to, but gods. Would he have put everything together sooner if he had been around the male more? Could he have stopped or changed any of this?

The iron door creaked, and one of the Marshals stuck his head out, a flickering torch in his hand. "What the fuck is going on out here? Don't you lot know it's the middle of the godsdamn night?" he grunted.

But that door opening was all Rayner needed. He moved among the smoke wafting up from the flames, appearing behind the Marshal, a dagger already pulled and slicing across the male's throat. He'd snatched the torch from his hand and was racing down the passageway before the Marshal's body had hit the ground.

He could hear them, the sounds of frightened people. He could smell the fear in the air. Moving again among the smoke, he left the torch behind and appeared in the large chamber where the stream filled a large pool. He materialized in the middle of a group of Marshals, two daggers leaving his hands and flying in opposite directions. Ducking when a sword came for him, he pulled a knife from his boot. He threw it, and the knife disappeared among ashes that swirled in his palm. He followed in another wisp of smoke, reappearing behind the swordsman. Rayner spun towards a large hearth along one wall of the chamber where the knife appeared in the ashes, still airborne from the force of his throw, lodging itself in the male's gut.

He heard more boots thundering down the passageway, and he moved to meet the guards, drawing his sword as he did. Arrows flew for him, but ashes were pouring out of one palm, creating a shield around him that the arrows bounced off of, clattering harmlessly to the ground. He lost track of how many guards he killed, the screams of frightened children and Fae echoing in the chamber. He couldn't stop. He couldn't stop until they were all dead, and Breya would be safe and—

"Rayner."

The sound of her voice had him spinning around to find her. How had she gotten down here so fast? But when his eyes landed on Moranna, his magic guttered. His shield fell away, bits of white ashes floating to the ground. She held a dagger in her hand, blood dripping off the end onto…

Onto the still form of a child with bright red hair lying in a growing pool of blood at her feet.

He'd dropped to his knees at some point, because suddenly Moranna's red painted nail was tipping up his chin, and he was staring into depthless dark eyes. She clicked her tongue at him, and a pitying pout formed on her lips. "Such poor choices, my Ash Rider."

"She was a child," he rasped, his eyes dropping back to the unmoving body.

"She was no longer of any use to me. Why would I feed and house something that is unable to offer me anything in return?" she replied, finger sliding along his jaw. "You've created quite the mess down here, Rayner. I cannot let this go unpunished."

He dragged his eyes back to her, but before he could reply, something was clamped onto his wrist. "Shirastone does not work on me," he snarled, jerking away from her touch.

"I know," she said soothingly. Then she leaned in closer to whisper into his ear, "That's why it is not shirastone."

He felt it then. The smothering of his magic. It was like shirastone but magnified by thousands. And the draining. Gods, he could feel his magic draining away. More than that, he could feel his very *life-force* draining away.

"What is the final count?" Moranna asked, straightening and taking a step back from him.

"Fifty-two," came the gruff voice of Feris.

She clicked her tongue again. "Fifty-two of my sentries and Marshals, Rayner. I am so disappointed."

His lip curled back, baring his elongated canines at her. "I am going to kill you. I am going to kill you and everyone who knew what was going on here and did nothing. I am to kill every Fae that followed your orders without questioning a fucking thing."

"And you, my pious Ash Rider?" Moranna asked, her arms folding and her chin resting on a thumb and forefinger. "You have killed on my orders. Did you question me?"

"You told me they deserved their deaths," he snapped.

"And they did. They would have drained valuable resources from the colony. Everything I do is to keep those in my charge well-taken care of. You know this," she replied placatingly.

"Where is Aravis?"

"Who?" she asked, her brow furrowing in feigned puzzlement. At his snarl, she continued, "Oh! The other child? She has been assigned as a power vessel. I already told you this." She stepped closer once more, bending down to speak softly to him again. Her fingers sank into his hair, her lips brushing the shell of his ear. "As soon as she has her first bleeding, she will be used until she is with child. She will bear many young for me. Surely one of them will be born as strong as you, not? I shall need *someone* to replace you in my bed one day." Her fingers tightened, tugging at his scalp. "But now, my Ash Rider, it is time to come back to bed."

"I will never bow to you again."

There were muffled gasps from the sentries still alive, and a low whistle came from Feris.

"Want him in a cell, your Grace?" the Captain asked, stepping to her side. He sneered down at him.

Moranna stood. "As much as it will hurt my heart to do so, perhaps that would be best for the remainder of the night," she agreed. "Give him one with a proper view of what you will finish carrying out tonight." She patted Rayner's cheek twice before moving to the opposite end of the chamber. Her palm pressed to the rocky wall, and an archway appeared, a set of stairs that wound up appearing. A hidden passageway. That's how she had made her way here so quickly.

Feris pulled him roughly to his feet, dragging him to a cell directly across from the pool and the boats tied to the wooden docks. A perfect view indeed.

The door clanged shut after he was shoved inside. Rayner felt wards sealing it up.

"The Baroness's favorite. Locked up. Can't say I haven't dreamed of this day, Ash Rider."

"I am sure it will be your favorite memory of me."

Feris snickered.

Rayner smiled back. A dark, wicked thing. The smile of a monster that had been awoken at the sight of Breya's lifeless body on the ground. "My favorite memory of you will be when I watch the life drain from your eyes while I hold your heart in the palm of my hand."

Feris stared back at him, blinking once, clearly unsure of how to respond to such a statement. Then he huffed a laugh. "I knew those swirling eyes meant you weren't all there, Ash Rider."

"You have no idea how true that statement is."

Feris didn't bother to reply, turning away and striding back to the remaining Marshals. There was a group of Fae, young and grown, huddled in the center of the chamber. Rayner counted them. Sixteen. Sixteen remained alive, while twelve were already dead.

Then he watched.

He watched as they drew daggers across throats. He watched every Fae fall to the ground, listened to every plea for mercy, and heard every cry of fear from a child. He watched as they filled the boats, and the Marshals boarded to ferry them outside the cliffs.

He watched as Breya was tossed thoughtlessly into the last boat. She would not be given a Farewell. None of them would. Her body might be burned, but she would not receive the rites of the Fire Court like she deserved.

He watched it all, taking in every detail, marking every face that would meet death at his hand. He let all of it feed the monster inside, let it all feed the growing appetite for vengeance. Not vengeance for him. Never for him. He should have done more long before tonight. He'd live with that guilt the rest of his life, however long or short that may be.

But as the chamber emptied and he was left in the silent dark, he made a vow that he would see Moranna dead before he left this world. He would see the entirety of the Southern Islands become a place that only the spirits visited, and even they would not want to linger after he was done with this place.

The sound of the iron door opening drew him from his thoughts. A Marshal appeared in front of his cell, his features shadowed in the flickering flames of the torch he held. He was one of the Marshals who had slaughtered Fae tonight. Rayner said nothing, staring back at him unblinkingly, contemplating which manner of death would suit him best.

"We do not have much time," the Fae said, his voice raspy, as though he rarely used it. When Rayner didn't move, he waved him over impatiently. "Come on, Ash Rider. That deathstone won't remove itself."

His eyes fell to the dark stone encircling his wrist. His wrist was bleeding where the stone was digging in. He hadn't felt a thing. He was numb. Numb to all of it except the rage coursing through him.

"You expect me to believe you are going to take it off of me?" Rayner asked. "I am not a fool."

"No, you are not," the Fae agreed. "You are the only one who can liberate those trapped here. I have waited decades for someone like you to show up."

Rayner's head tilted to the side. "I watched you butcher innocent Fae tonight."

The Fae swallowed audibly, nodding once.

Rayner smiled at him. "If you take this off, I will end you."

Even in the sparse torchlight, he could see the male pale. "It— It will be nothing less I deserve."

Rayner pushed to his feet, drifting towards the shirastone bars. He gripped them in his hands, leaning down to peer into the male's face. The male took a small step back. "Explain what you mean when you say you have been waiting for someone like me to show up."

The male nodded. "There are few powerful enough to take on the Baroness. The ones who are do not wish to. They like the power they have here, but you… You are different. You will do what I would never be able to."

"You could have stopped killing at any moment," Rayner sneered.

"Only to meet my own death. And then what? I would just be replaced."

"But you would not have so much blood on your hands."

The male hung his head. "I am prepared for you to take my life when I free you, Ash Rider. I will face Arius's judgment and spend my eternity in the Pits of Torment knowing I deserve every moment."

Rayner looked the male up and down before meeting his eyes once more. Then he shoved his arm through the bars. With a shaking hand, the Marshal slipped the stone from his wrist. In the next breath, Rayner had moved through the smoke of the torch. The male didn't have a chance to scream as a blade went through his back and pierced his heart.

"Consider a quick death a mercy," Rayner said, his tone low and dark. "For surely Arius will not grant you any."

He let the male fall to the ground, the torch hissing as it went out, rolling across the stone. Rayner didn't need it. He had excellent eyesight in the dark. The minute he was past the iron door, he was moving among the smoke again. He would leave the cliffs, regroup, and then come back for Aravis once his power had fully replenished.

He made his way to the front entry hall, still planning to kill those five sentries before he left, but he drew up short when he found Moranna standing in the archway that would lead outside.

"More unwise choices, Rayner," she chided, her hand clasped around something he could not see. He reached over his shoulder for his sword, but she tutted at him. "Now, now, before you make another unwise choice, let me speak. Should you attempt to take my life, Aravis will be thrown from the top levels."

Rayner spun to find she was not bluffing. He could make out two figures at the railing of one of the top levels. "What are your terms?" he demanded, turning back to Moranna.

"I thought you would see things my way," she simpered, moving towards him. "Give me some of your blood, and I will let you leave these islands. I will not stop you."

"What else?"

She shrugged. "That is it."

"And Aravis?"

"Oh, she must stay."

"I will come back for her."

"I am sure you will," she purred. "Should you make the choice to stay now, I am afraid both of your lives will be forfeit. Which would be…unfortunate."

Knowing this was surely a trap, but not seeing any way around it, he nodded. Moranna jerked her chin, and a sentry hurried from the shadows. Rayner's eyes never left hers as the sentry filled five vials with his blood. When he was done, he dropped his arm to his side, the wound already healing.

Moranna stepped to the side, gesturing towards the exit. "As agreed."

Rayner moved forward, waiting for the catch. He turned so he could keep her in his sight, refusing to turn his back on her. He paused as the archway began to shimmer, the beach appearing on the other side. "Your death is mine, Moranna. I am coming for you and everyone here."

"I await your return home," she said with a small smile. "But know that when you cross those wards this night, you shall not remember how to get back here. You will lose all your memories of your time here. I wonder, how will you find your way to someplace you do not even know exists?"

"I have never had such a problem before," he snarled.

"But you always came back to me, Rayner," she replied. "You had reason to return, and I had reason to want you to. Now I have reason to keep you away for a time, to make you pay for what you have done here this night. How dreadful to not remember anything about your past. To not know where you come from. You will not even remember you had kin, let alone remember to return for one."

"I swear to you, I will be your end."

"We shall see, my Ash Rider."

"I am not your Ash Rider, Moranna, but I will your end."

And with that, he stepped through the archway, breathing in the sea air before everything went black.

CHAPTER I

T hey had gotten smarter since the last time he had visited the islands. The last time he was here, nearly four decades ago, the guards outside the cliff's entrance had a fire burning to ward off the night chill from the sea. Rayner had appeared among the smoke and had all five of them lying in pools of blood before they had realized what had happened.

This time he'd had to move among the thick vegetation. He'd assumed they wouldn't make that mistake again, and when he returned this time, he'd come in on merchant ships. It had been two weeks at sea departing from the Water Court. He could have traveled among ashes, but he knew better than to underestimate Moranna, even after all these years.

But she would always wait for him to come to her.

After coming to the islands every few years when he'd finally regained his lost memories, he'd purposefully waited decades this round. He let them relax, lulled them into a false sense of safety. But he'd been just as busy on the continent. It had happened by chance the first time. He'd recognized an overseer in a market in the Shifter territory. A good hour in an abandoned building and a few calculated stab wounds had the male telling Rayner all he needed to know. Moranna's superiors were moving people out because of the destruction he was causing. Many of the guards and overseers had been spread to various positions throughout the continent. The male hadn't known what exactly everyone was doing, but some had been assigned as spies in various territories. He had been one of those spies. The male had eventually died of suffocation.

From smoke inhalation.

And Rayner had found himself with a new purpose while planning his missions to the Southern Islands. He'd promised he would kill every single one of the people who had helped to keep the innocent people trapped in the cliffs, and he had suddenly found his hunting grounds expanded. He knew he'd become a rumor, a being as mythical as the Oracle. But people did not refer to him as the Ash Rider. No, he was whispered about as The Reaper, as if saying the name too loudly would summon him.

The last time he'd come to the Southern Islands, he'd nearly been caught. Arrows with shirastone tips. It didn't stop his gifts, but they still hurt like hell when lodged in one's kidney and caused sloppy movements. He'd managed to get a group of twenty-five out, half of them children. It was the most he'd ever moved out at one time. When he'd left, he'd estimated there were still at least two hundred innocents left in the colony, but that number would be higher now. Lots of younglings could be born in forty years, and he would guess the Baroness was a little more *tolerant* of those with lower power levels, considering her dwindling pool of subjects.

It was helping, he supposed, in one way. She allowed more to live, thus keeping them safe until he could come back for them. Although, safe probably wasn't the best word to use. It kept them alive, which was better than dead…for most of them.

Despite that upside, there was the issue that Moranna had moved her most prized and most powerful. They were kept locked away and hidden, and he knew that would include Aravis if she was still alive.

He'd had yet to figure out where exactly Moranna had stowed them away though. Which is why he had waited all these years. He wanted the sentries to have their guard down. He had no intention of making his presence known this time. There was only one Fae he had his sights set on for this visit.

The Captain of the Marshals.

Fortunately for the guards outside the cliffs, that meant they would get to keep their lives this visit if all went according to plan. He crept from the thick expanse of trees and plants, smoke drifting from a small torch he kept smoldering. He was several hundred feet away from the entrance into the city beneath the cliffs. It was the only place a person could walk in and out, the brand that was given beneath their skin when they were born their key to enter. He lifted a hand, ashes pouring from his palm and seeking the wards surrounding the place. He'd once thought he could only move among existing smoke and ashes. It wasn't until he had remembered his training from this cursed place that he learned he could create his own. It drained his reserves far too fast to do it regularly though.

But he'd learned even more about his gifts since his time spent inside the cliff walls. Things he had been more than happy to share with those who kept the innocents trapped here like slaves. Like how he could control which parts of him shifted to ash. How he could send those ashes into a body, wrap them around hearts or lungs or bones.

Ashes swirled halfway up the cliff-side, and Rayner's lips kicked up in a wicked grin. One of her failsafes. Moranna always left one small weak spot in her wards to make her own escape if necessary. She'd gotten clever with them since he'd left, but not clever enough. In the next breath, he was hovering above the ground in his ashes. The next blink, he was inside.

He immediately disappeared among the smoke of the sconces lining the wall. Nothing had changed. Everything was still pristine and white, spelled to always look that way. She still made Fae clean every day, saying they needed to earn their keep, as if being bred like prized livestock wasn't enough.

Rage coursed through his veins at the thought, the monster she'd created lifting its head. His ashes trembled beneath his skin, as hungry for violence as he was. He breathed deep, the scent of smoke and fire filling his senses, fueling the surging anticipation inside.

Staying hidden, he flitted among the braziers, taking in everything happening. With the ward breech halfway up, he was on the mid-levels. Everything was quiet, Fae hurrying along when they passed, eyes fixed to the floor. The white clothing everyone was issued blended in with the walls, the floor, everything. The only color in the place had been Moranna in her bright red attire.

Until he'd returned and added a little color of his own with blood splatters on the walls and pools of it on the floor, corpses left in his wake. He'd glimpsed Moranna once in all the times he'd come back to these cursed cliffs. She'd appeared on the highest level the third time he'd come back, staring down at him, a faint smile on her red painted lips. He'd only been a few levels below her, so he'd heard the words when she'd said, "Welcome home, my Ash Rider."

By the time he'd moved through the smoke to reach her, she'd disappeared. He'd had to choose between going after her or getting the group of Fae he'd already gathered out. If he went after Moranna, those Fae were surely dead, so he'd left her for another time.

He maneuvered up through the levels. Feris had been housed on the same level his own rooms had been on when Rayner had resided here. It would be easy enough to see if that was still the case. He was nearing the top when a scream made him stop mid-leap between ashes. Smoke swirled when he stepped from it, his boots silent on the pristine floor. Calculating what level he was on, he realized this was either on a floor of producing rooms or a level where some of the more powerful used to be housed.

Keeping to the walls to avoid being seen along the railings, Rayner moved quickly, straining to pick up any other sounds. The walls were thick rock, and the doors were solid wood. To be heard through them, the scream had to have been roaring. He sent his ashes from his palm as he went, seeping under the cracks of the doors and seeking any sign of sentience. His ashes, usually associated with death, always reacted differently to life. They would vibrate, strain to get closer; whether curious or seeking to destroy, he was never quite sure. But when they trembled and pulled him closer to one of the last rooms, he knew they'd found something.

Pulling them back into himself, Rayner pushed the door open, feeling the wards crackle over his skin. Just as shirastone did not affect him, he was able to pass through most wards without issue. But when he stepped across the threshold, he stilled, taking in the scene before him. This was a producing room all right, but this was not one of Moranna's assignments.

This was sentries and overseers taking what they wanted.

His lip curled back, his ashes vibrating beneath his skin for an entirely different reason now. But he still didn't move. Because one overseer, the one closest to the female, was on the ground.

An arrow shoved into his eye.

Where the arrow had come from, Rayner didn't know. There was no bow in sight and no other arrows. Just the one protruding from the man's face.

He lay there, moaning and cursing, yelling at the other two males in the room to get the arrow out. But they stood frozen against the wall, and Rayner was fairly certain it wasn't because of him.

The female was young. He was certain she hadn't gone through her Staying yet. Her long, black hair was braided into a plait over her shoulder, and she wore a black gown, not the usual white attire. She was on the shorter side and barefoot, and when his gaze connected with hers, amber eyes stared back at him. Not that she could see him beneath his hood, but her wide eyes told him she knew exactly who he was.

"You...are the Reaper," she whispered. Rayner said nothing. "I did not think you were real. I thought…" She trailed off, but Rayner was already focusing on the males in the room.

"Did you do this?" Rayner asked.

She hesitated before answering. "…yes."

"Are you hurt?"

"No."

Rayner nodded, advancing farther into the room. "Get out of here. All the way out if you can. There is a merchant ship leaving in an hour that will take you to the continent if you can make it to the ship in time. Take others with you if you can. The guards are about to be preoccupied."

He hadn't looked at her again, his attention fixed on the still whimpering overseer, but he felt her make her way across the room, felt her pause beside him.

"They have made preparations for your return," she said softly.

"Close the door behind you."

When it thudded shut, he moved to stand next to the overseer. His attention shifted to the other two sentries. "Do not try to run."

They both nodded, and he heard one audibly gulp as he lowered to a crouch beside the overseer. His hands were still on his face, smearing blood across his brow and cheeks.

Rayner reached for the arrow, but the male shrieked, "No!"

He paused, fingers an inch from the arrow shaft. "Were you not just screaming at your companions to remove it?"

The male blubbered, incoherent mumblings coming from his lips, and before he could sense the movement, Rayner snatched the arrow, tugging it from the man's eye socket. The organ itself was attached to the arrowhead, and the sound of it popping free had one of the sentries behind him retching.

And the other one running.

Moving through the smoke from the lit torches on either side of the doorway, Rayner materialized in front of the sentry. He tried to backtrack, his boots slipping across the floor. Before the male could beg,

Rayner's hand was nothing but ashes, reaching into the man's leg. Fingers of ash closed around bone, and the male's screams filled the room when Rayner tore it from his limb. He tossed it to the side. It clattered on the stone, blood and sinew splattering. The male was already on the floor, and Rayner lowered down in front of him to peer at his face. Tears were tracking down pale cheeks, spittle dripping from his chin as he clutched at his leg.

"I told you not to run," Rayner said, his tone low and icy. "If you try to drag yourself out of this room, I will remove every bone from your body and make sure you feel it all."

The male nodded emphatically, trying and failing to quiet himself. Still holding the arrow in his other hand, Rayner moved back to the overseer, crouching beside him once more.

"Were you going to be the first to rape her?" Rayner asked, twirling the arrow between his thumb and forefinger after he removed the now useless organ from the end of it. The man only whimpered. "Tell you what. You answer a riddle; I let you keep your other eye."

A puddle slowly formed beneath the male, the smell of piss mingling with the raw terror in the air.

"What is a dreamer's lie?" he asked casually, placing the tip of the arrow over the male's heart. He could hear it beating too rapidly. The male whimpered again, trembling violently now. "Quickly. I have others to tend to."

The male's mouth opened and closed, gaping like a fish out of water. "I— I don't… I don't know," he gasped as Rayner slid the arrow up his chest and along his throat.

Rayner leaned in close, whispering into his ear as the arrow pressed along his cheekbone just enough to draw a thin line of blood. "A dreamer's lie is that all nightmares have an end." Another strangled cry. "The truth is, some nightmares go on forever, and yours is just beginning."

The sound of more retching mingled with the screams when he brought the arrow down again, taking the male's other eye. Rayner was doing him a favor really. He wouldn't be able to see all the ways he was about to make him bleed. Then again, without his sight, the sensations would be intensified. Maybe it wasn't a favor after all.

By the time his attention shifted to the one sentry who wasn't bleeding, the two other males were no longer breathing. He stood from dealing with the one now missing not only a leg bone, but a couple ribs, and a few vital organs. The remaining sentry had sunk to the floor, piles of vomit off to one side. He was pale and trembling, staring up at Rayner when he moved to stand in front of him. The male closed his eyes, seeming to brace for the agony he'd witnessed his companions go through.

"I have some questions for you," Rayner said.

"I will answer them," he gasped out. "I will do whatever you ask in order to live."

"Who said anything about you living?" Rayner asked, pulling a dagger from beneath his cloak. "Answer my questions, and I will give you a quicker death than your companions received. But keeping your life is not on the table." Rayner thought the male might be sick yet again judging by the way he somehow paled even more. "Feris. Are his rooms still on the upper level?"

"The Captain? Yes. Two levels below the Baroness."

"These preparations the female mentioned. What are they?"

"I don't know."

Rayner struck, snapping one of the male's fingers back. The male howled, clutching his hand to his chest. "That was not the answer I was looking for," Rayner growled.

Tears were leaking from the male's eyes, beads of sweat forming on his brow. "I don't know," he sobbed. "I am not high-ranking enough to know such details."

"But high-ranking enough to take from the females? Somehow I doubt that."

"I swear it," he cried, trying to press back from him more.

"Lie to me again, and I take a kneecap," Rayner snarled, lifting a hand and letting it fade into ashes.

"I don't know!" the male cried again. "I don't know what they have planned for you! I oversee the younglings! That's my job!"

Rayner paused. "Explain."

"The Baroness is moving them. Taking them off the islands. My job is to ready the young on transport days," the sentry said.

"Transport them were?"

"I'm not told that. I take them to a transporting room on the main level."

Transporting room? That was new. There had never been such a thing when Rayner had resided here.

"Aravis. Do you know who she is?" Rayner demanded.

"I do not know that name," the sentry said, shaking his head.

"She has been here for over a century. Black hair. Grey eyes. Fire gifts," Rayner said. "The Baroness would keep her close by."

"Her most guarded are hidden away. Only a few know where," the sentry replied, his trembling seeming to have lessened as they spoke.

"Who else would know besides Feris?"

Dread filled the male's pale blue eyes. "I don't know," he whispered.

"Then you are no longer of use to me."

Rayner's dagger slashed across the male's throat. He left him there, choking on his own blood. A quicker death than his companions had received, as promised.

He stepped from the room, moving up a few more levels to the housing block where Feris's quarters would be. Ashes flitted from his fingertips, drifting along the floor, seeking life or death. He passed what was once his quarters, continuing on to the other end of the level.

And when his ashes started buzzing in anticipation, a cold smile formed on Rayner's lips.

He had a favorite memory to make.

CHAPTER 2

T he fire burning in Feris's hearth was more than enough for
Rayner to materialize inside his rooms. He took in the space.
Dirty uniforms crumpled in a heap in the corner. Unmade
bed. Weapons discarded haphazardly across a desk.

He could hear him moving around in the bathing room, and
Rayner swiped up one of his daggers, examining it. Shirastone. The
upper level guards were each issued one. The other weapons were of
standard make. Steel and practical.

He leaned back against the desk, lifting a palm. Smoke swirled, the
arrow from the producing room appearing in his hand. He held it up,
studying the arrowhead. That was not shirastone. It was darker, seeming
to absorb light. Memories of the same material digging into his skin when
he was in a cell flashed in his mind. The Marshal who had let him out
had called it deathstone, but Rayner had never seen it on weapons when
he was here. Unless this was one way they had prepared for his return.

The sound of shuffling feet told him Feris was coming. Rayner
didn't even bother to look up. When he heard the muffled curse
though, he slowly raised his head, peering out from beneath his hood.

Feris stared back at him, hatred shining in his eyes. "The favorite returns," he spat.

"Am I still the favorite?" Rayner questioned, reaching up and pulling back the hood. He wanted Feris to see his face. Wanted him to know he had come to collect the memory he had promised to make. "That doesn't say much about you. I have been gone for decades, and you still haven't managed to take my place."

"The Baroness has plans for you," Feris snarled, but it sounded more like he was reminding himself. Rayner had no doubt Moranna had issued orders about what to do with him if he showed up, and those orders did not include Feris killing him.

"I have plans for her as well, but first I need some information," Rayner said.

"Fuck off, Ash Rider. If you think I'm going to tell you shit, think again."

Rayner only smiled. Holding his stare, he tossed the arrow up. Ashes swirled around it, and when it reappeared, it went through the back of Feris's shoulder.

He bellowed out a curse, trying to grab the thing, but it was lodged just out of his reach.

"That is quite the weapon," Rayner said casually. "Are there more?"

"It is deathstone, you fucking prick. We do not have weapons with it." His face was turning a mottled red from pain and anger.

Rayner sent him a frank look. "Do not lie to me, Feris."

"I'm not." His lip curled back, but it quickly morphed from a sneer to a grimace. "She only has a few items of deathstone. Arrows are not one of them."

"Then where did it come from?"

"You tell me. You are the one who possesses such a thing."

Rayner studied him as he continued to struggle to reach the arrow. He was almost inclined to believe that he did not know where the arrow had come from, which opened up a whole new set of questions. It couldn't have simply appeared out of nowhere.

"What preparations have been made?" Rayner asked in a low voice.

"Fuck. Off," Feris ground out again from between his teeth.

Rayner sighed, pushing off the desk and prowling forward. The male's lip peeled back, elongated canines bared, but the arrow was suppressing his earth magic. He was also weaponless, having clearly just come from bathing. Sloppy. Rayner always had a dagger or knife within reach, even in the bath. Feris was just as arrogant as ever, his next words only solidifying that fact.

"Go ahead and kill me, Ash Rider. I'm not going to tell you a gods-damn thing."

Rayner lifted a hand, flesh becoming ashes. "You won't be meeting death until I say so, Feris, and that will not happen until I have the information I need."

His hand snapped out, sinking deep into his throat where fingers of ash wrapped around his windpipe, squeezing. Feris's eyes bulged, Rayner's favorite look of panic settling into his cold eyes. He abandoned his attempt to reach the arrow, now clawing at his neck, mouth gaping.

"When I allow you to take a breath, I expect to hear what preparations have been made for me. If that is not what I hear from your mouth, you will learn a few more of my new talents."

He eased his grip, pulling his hand back and wiping it on his cloak. Feris sucked in breaths, gasping, "You twisted fuck."

And Rayner's ashes sang as they sank into the length of Feris's arm. They expanded, layering along the bones, muscles, veins…and then they sank in even further, turning it all to ash. Feris screamed, feeling every bit of desecration.

He pulled his magic back, keeping a grimace from his face. His magic reserves were starting to deplete. He needed to make sure he had enough magic left to get back to the continent, so he really needed

Feris to start sharing some secrets.

The male opened his mouth, but before he could speak, Rayner said, "The words you are about to say had better be how she has prepared for me."

"She has an enchantment on the islands. The entirety of them," Feris rasped, beads of sweat running down his brow. He was staring at his boneless arm, and Rayner snapped his fingers in his face to keep him from going into any type of shock.

"How?"

"I don't know, but she knows when you come. Every time. She knows you are here now."

"Then why hasn't she come for me?"

"She's not ready for you yet."

Whatever the fuck that meant.

Rayner didn't have time to waste on this now. He had other things he needed to know, then he needed to get the fuck out of here while he still had the power to do so.

"The most powerful. Where does she keep them?"

Something hardened on Feris's face as though he were going to decline to answer, but Rayner merely needed to lift his hand again, ashes drifting from his fingers, and Feris was blurting, "In one of her secret chambers. I haven't seen them since she moved them there."

Interesting.

"Aravis. Where is she being kept?"

At that, something sinister crept across Feris's face. "When she's not fulfilling her assignments, she warms my bed, Ash Rider."

A snarl of rage left Rayner as his hand plunged into Feris's chest. This time, he didn't leave it as ashes. He let his flesh reform, solid fingers wrapping around Feris's heart.

The male gasped, face contorted in agony, but he still managed to say, "She let me take her for the first time. Let me teach her how to prepare for her duties. And she will use her to claim you once more."

He bellowed a roar of pain when Rayner sank a dagger deep into his side, twisting sharply. "Arius will welcome you into the Pits of Torment," Rayner snarled.

"You will be in the Pits with the rest of us," Feris rasped between ragged breaths as Rayner's fingers tightened around his heart.

"I'm counting on it," Rayner replied. "I will find you there and finish what I started here."

He ripped his hand back, Feris's heart in his palm. Blood bubbled from the male's lips as he sank to the floor, and Rayner watched the life drain from his eyes before he tossed his heart atop the body and disappeared among the smoke.

He'd been right. That would forever be one of his fondest memories.

CHAPTER 3

He took a drink from his mug of ale. This was one of the more rundown taverns in Solembra. It was tucked into a back alley on the edges of the capital city, and it was frequented by some rather questionable patrons. But they had the best ale in the Fire Court, and he was one of those questionable patrons, so Rayner found it rather suitable. He had to hand it to the prince of this Court. While this might be one of the more shady establishments in the city, he'd seen much worse throughout the continent. But even the Fire Prince couldn't keep every corner of his lands neat and tidy and perfect. It was a far cry from the legends of the Black Syndicate, but thieves and cheats and hirelings still found their way in.

He was a prime example.

He had a small house located farther into the city, closer to the markets and businesses. The Fire Court seemed the natural place to have a home, if he could even call it that. When he spent too much of his magic, it was where he recovered. Like he had been doing for the last two seasons. It's where he planned and plotted when he wasn't off wandering to the farthest reaches of the continent trying to track down answers. He'd had a house on the outside of the city at one point. A small estate with room to run.

He'd sold it as soon as he'd remembered he owned it.

Decades. It had taken him decades to overcome the enchantment Moranna had put on him when he'd left the cliffs on the Southern Islands. He'd wasted so much godsdamn coin on false seers and Witches who swore they could brew up a tonic to bring back his memories. He'd found it a better use of his time to live among the smoke and ashes and pick up on rumors throughout the various kingdoms, then follow the rumors to see if they were true. Even that had been largely a waste of his time.

Until the day he found his way to the Oracle.

He paused to catch his breath. This was stupid. Foolish and idiotic and stupid to try to get through the Witch Kingdoms without alerting any of the Covens. The High Witch had eyes and ears everywhere. He was running out of ashes and smoke too. Once he cleared this small town, he would be hiking to the cliff cave.

And hopefully avoiding any run-ins with the Witches.

He took another few moments to breathe deep and let his heart rate settle before he set off again, flitting between the smoke billowing from the houses of the village. The ashes of a fire pit a few miles out let him get a little farther than anticipated, but here was where his magic wouldn't be of much use for traveling.

He fingered a few of the small medallions in his pocket. He'd wasted a lot of coin on false Witches, but these had actually come in handy. They had been created by magic, so he was able to imbue them with some of his own. He stored ashes in them, allowing him to throw them and move among the ashes released if there were no smoke or ashes around to move through. If he ran into a Witch, he'd need all the advantages he could get.

He pulled a map from a pocket realm, looking it over before folding it up and tucking into the pocket of his cloak. Detailed maps of the Witch Kingdoms were nearly impossible to find. Another thing he'd paid an obscene amount of coin for, and it wasn't even a decent one. It had simply been better than any other map he'd ever come across.

Knowing it was foolish to linger too long in one spot when he did not have permission to be in these lands, Rayner set off at a brisk pace. The grey skies only added to the chill of the territory. There wasn't snow on the ground, but frost still clung to everything.

There were various rumors about where to find the mythical Oracle. Too many rumors to ever try and substantiate them all. Some were ridiculous, but some he'd looked into. Most had led to dead ends, but a few had paid off. Bits and pieces of a few rumors woven together over the last few decades were how he'd finally figured out where she was.

Or where he hoped she was (if it was a she), because if this turned out to be a complete waste of his fucking time and he had to start over from scratch, he wasn't entirely sure what he would do.

He stepped from a copse of ancient trees at the base of the cliffs when he heard it. The screech of an eagle.

Except it wasn't an eagle.

It was a griffin.

Fuck.

He slipped a medallion from his pocket, clenching it in his fist while he kept moving. He didn't make it very far. The griffin dove, hard and fast. If he tried to make a run for it, Rayner knew he'd find more than one arrow in his back. His only real option was to stop and pray to Anala the Witch would escort him to the border.

The ground beneath his boots shook when the beast landed fifteen feet away from him, its rider slipping from its back. And as she stalked towards him, drawing her sword from her back, he knew he was well and truly fucked.

Hazel Hecate. The High Witch.

She stopped in front of him, her blade leveled at his throat. "Lower your hood," she ordered in an icy tone, violet eyes burning into him.

"I would rather not," he replied, fingers itching to reach for his own weapons.

"It was not a request."

Keeping the medallion in hand, he slowly lifted his arms, pushing back the hood of his cloak. If the High Witch was surprised by the swirling smoke in his eyes, she did not show it.

"I have heard rumors one of you had been spotted on the continent."

"I have heard rumors the Oracle resides in your kingdom," Rayner countered.

The High Witch's lip curled slightly in disgust. "Do you know what we do to males in my lands, Ash Rider?"

"I do."

"And yet here you stand."

Rayner did not answer. Just held her gaze, waiting to see what she did next.

She slowly lowered her sword, holding it at her side. "There has not been an Ash Rider born in centuries."

"That you were aware of."

"What business do you have with the Oracle?"

"None of yours."

Her head tilted. A predator assessing prey. "Tell me, Ash Rider, do you value your tongue?"

"I find it useful," he conceded.

"Then I suggest you mind how you speak to me." She took a step towards him. "I do not care if you are the last Ash Rider that will ever walk this realm. I will not hesitate to take you from this world for male arrogance."

"I meant no disrespect, Lady," Rayner replied. "Truly."

"What is in your hand?"

"A trinket."

"Show me."

He opened his fist, showing her the medallion. She held out her own hand, and he begrudgingly dumped the medallion into it. She held it up between two fingers, studying it intensely, before she slipped it into a pocket of her witchsuit. "I will take you to the Oracle."

It took everything in him to not show the shock that rippled through him. "Why?"

"The Oracle told me one would come with such a trinket. When he did, I was to show him the way." She turned, sheathing her sword down her back as she added, "It is the only reason you are not dead." Rayner watched her walk back to her grif-

fin, the beast lowering to the ground at her approach so she could hoist herself onto its back. When its large wings flared wide, preparing to take to the sky, the High Witch said, "Meet me where you see him land."

Rayner stood on the edge of the copse and watched the creature soar up, climbing higher and higher. It was several minutes before it banked to land somewhere well over halfway up the side of the cliffs. Which was…fucking great.

Gritting his teeth, he pulled the cloak hood back into place. Even though no one was around and the High Witch knew who he was, he felt far too exposed when his hood wasn't hiding him from the rest of the world.

It took hours to climb up the cliff side. If it weren't for the healing capabilities of the Fae, he would have arrived there with bloodied palms and numerous bruises. The rocks were covered with the same frost that glistened on the purple and turquoise leaves of the ancient trees, making them difficult to climb even with the extra grips on the soles of his boots.

The High Witch was standing next to an entrance to a cave when he finally pulled himself over the lip of a ledge, her griffin perched on rocks a little higher up. His golden eyes were fixed on Rayner, lion's tail swishing back and forth. The feathers on his wings ruffled slightly, and he clicked his beak when Rayner moved towards his master. Beside the High Witch sat a small stone table, a vial atop it.

"You are not permitted to take weapons in with you," the High Witch said. "You can retrieve them when the Oracle releases you."

Releases him? That sounded…promising. But he'd come this far, and he needed answers, so he again found himself without much of a choice.

After removing the various weapons strapped to his body and setting them aside, the High Witch gestured towards the vial. "This will temporarily nullify your gifts. The Oracle will give them back when you have heard what you need to."

Without letting himself think about it, Rayner swiped up the vial and downed the contents. He instantly felt empty, void of the ashes that drifted in his veins. He knew if he could see his eyes, they would be an unmoving grey. No swirling with the telltale sign of what he was.

"See what awaits," the High Witch said, motioning to the cave mouth. He took a step, but she called out, "And Ash Rider?"

Looking back over his shoulder, he said, "Yes?"

"You would do well to be out of my lands by dawn."

"Understood, my Lady."

The High Witch nodded once to him, and he turned back to the cave. He knew she'd be long gone whenever he emerged, but someone would be watching him to make sure he was indeed across their borders when the sun next rose.

He entered the cave, navigating the pitch black interior. Even with his Fae sight, he could not see a thing. His gifts had always given him an extra advantage due to his need to move through smoke. Without that gift, he felt blind. Fingers gliding along the rocky wall, he moved down the passageway. It only took a few minutes before a glow appeared up ahead, and when he stepped through, he blinked in surprise at what he found.

No one knew the Oracle's true form. It was said she appeared differently to each person who came to her. But why he was staring at a child, he had no idea.

The girl had to be no older than seven with bright red hair and freckles across her nose and cheeks, but her violet eyes held a depth and knowing to them that told Rayner she was far, far older than she appeared. The girl wore a simple dress, feet bare where she stood on the dirt-covered cave floor, and Rayner had the strangest feeling that he knew this child. He could not place her though, no matter how hard he tried.

"And so the one with many names has finally found his way to me," the little girl said, watching him carefully, hands clasped behind her back.

"You are a child?" Rayner asked without thinking, still trying to figure out how he knew her face.

"I am many things to many people. I am whatever you need me to be," she answered, her voice small and innocent.

"And I need you to be…a child? Why?"

"Why indeed."

Rayner reached up, pushing back his hood, suddenly unconcerned with being too exposed in the Oracle's presence. *"The High Witch said you have been waiting for me,"* he said hoarsely, not liking how much the sight of a child was throwing him off balance.

"I have been," she agreed, her head tilting slightly. *"But I did not know if it*

would be the Ash Rider who found their way to me or one of the many other titles you go by or will go by."

"You are the Oracle. How could you not know?"

A faint smile appeared on her lips. "Fate is constantly changing. Every choice one makes alters what is to come, which means every future I glimpse is only one possibility." She began to move, leaving small footprints in the dirt as she circled him. "What do you seek from me?"

"My memories," he answered. "My past. I do not... My earliest memory is from nearly six decades ago. I know nothing of my life before that."

"No," the girl said, shaking her head. "That is not what you seek."

Unsure of what to say to that, he watched for a few silent moments before he said, "That is all I have sought since I found myself on a beach in the Water Court, unaware of how I arrived there."

"That is what you think *you have been seeking," she corrected, disappearing into the shadows of the cave where he could no longer see her.*

Rayner spun, her voice coming from behind him now. "Then what is it you think I have been seeking?"

"Why do you seek these lost memories?"

"Who wouldn't want to know where they came from?"

"What does it matter?" the voice countered, coming from his left this time. "Will your past decide your future?"

"Maybe."

"Why?" The question was full of a child's curiosity.

"Why? Why wouldn't it?"

"Will it define who you are?"

"I already know I am an Ash Rider."

"That is what *you are. Not who you are. And even then..." Rayner whirled, the voice coming from another spot in the cave now. "Even then, that is not entirely what you are. You are more than ash and smoke. You are more than Fae. But none of that is who you are. So many names in your past. So many names in your future." She stepped from the shadows, a slightly terrifying smile on her small face. "Ash Rider. Wanderer. Favorite." She slipped back into the dark, stepping from somewhere new that had Rayner spinning around yet again. "Reaper."*

"Reaper?"

Her smile tipped up even more, her head tilting. "Brother."

"Brother?" he repeated in a slightly horrified whisper.

"Would you like to know some other names that could be yours?"

"I…" He paused. Did he want to know? "No, I just want to know what lies in my past."

"Why?"

Frustration coursed through him. "Because how can I know who I am if I do not know where I came from?"

Her smile widened, and she stepped right up to him, her bare toes touching his boots. Her head was tipped back, and she spoke softly when she said, "That is what you seek, Ash Rider. Not your memories. Not your past. You wish to know who you are, who you are supposed to be."

Rayner flinched back when several torches burst to light, flames flickering and casting shadows along the cave walls. The child moved to a stone table that appeared in the center of the room, a basin atop it. She climbed upon the table, stirring the contents with her fingers.

"One not of this world took from you. Took more than your memories." She looked up, violet eyes connecting with his where he still stood across the chamber. "Understand that if I give these memories back to you, there is no undoing it. Consider that sometimes it is better to not know than to live with memories you cannot change. Consider that maybe losing these memories was a blessing rather than a curse. And consider that learning such secrets of your past still may not tell you who you are."

"Do you know what these memories are?" he asked.

"No," she answered. She reached into the basin, and when she pulled her hand back out, a vial was held between her fingers. "Make your choice, descendant of Anala and those who hunt."

"What does that mean?"

"There is so much more to your gifts than you know. So many futures," the child mused. "I wonder which will come to pass."

· · ·

40

He'd taken the vial, and the moment he'd swallowed down the elixir, the entirety of his first three decades came flooding back to him. The Southern Islands. The cliffs. Moranna. Feris. Aravis. Breya.

He'd sank to his knees when he realized the Oracle's form was that of his youngest sister who he'd been unable to save.

But he'd left the cave with a new title.

The Reaper.

That's what he had become. His sole purpose had become freeing the innocents still trapped in the cliffs, hoping he was not too late to save Aravis.

Rayner signaled the barkeep to bring him another mug of ale as he watched the Fae around him. A shady game of cards was happening in a dark corner. One deck of playing cards had already gone up in flames. He would bet this deck would go up within the next hour. A few females were off to one side, scoping out their options. Some for pleasure, some for coin. He knew if he lowered the hood of his cloak, one would approach within minutes. It was why he kept the hood up.

Well, one of the reasons.

The other was as soon as people saw his eyes swirling with the ashes and smoke, they quickly realized what he was, and that always brought about a gambit of reactions. Some wanted to employ him. Some wanted to fuck him. Some wanted to fight him. All of them annoyed him.

Which is why he snarled a warning when the barkeep brought his mug of ale over and someone else dropped some coin onto his table to cover his tab.

"Do not accept that," Rayner growled, reaching for his own coin. He didn't even bother to look at whoever was attempting to buy him a drink. He didn't incur debts, and he didn't accept favors or kind gestures. Such things always ended up turning into debts in the end.

The barkeep glanced from him to whoever was standing at the table, wiping his hands nervously on his apron. "Sorry, sire," he finally answered. "I must accept it," he added, quickly swiping up the coin and bowing before he scurried away.

The bowing was perplexing.

Until someone slid into the chair across from him. Then it made perfect sense.

Bright amber eyes stared back at him, soot black hair falling over his brow. He wore a dark red short-sleeved tunic, gold and copper threads embroidered along the collar. The male braced his forearms on the table, a faint arrogant smirk tilting on his lips.

The Prince of the Fire Court.

CHAPTER 4

Rayner wasn't sure what he had done to garner the attention of the Fire Prince, but he knew better than to speak first in these types of situations. If he was going to be accused of something, he didn't want to implicate himself for the wrong thing. If he was going to be asked something, he didn't want to give any illusion that he was the type of male that took part in friendly conversation.

"You are an incredibly difficult Fae to track down," the Fire Prince said, that arrogant smirk kicking up even more.

Rayner didn't say anything in reply. Just continued to stare at him from beneath his hood. He twisted in his seat at the sound of another chair being dragged over before a female plopped unceremoniously into it. She huffed loudly, crossing her arms, a red-gold braid hanging over her shoulder.

"How do you even know it is him?" the female drawled, signaling the barkeep for a mug of ale.

"I have eyes in my city," the prince answered, golden eyes still fixed on Rayner.

He held in his scoff of amusement. *Eyes in his city*. Fae were naturally stealthy. Light on their feet. Keen senses. But few could move as he did. Few could hide in the ashes and hear things not meant to be overheard. Only the Wind Walkers were comparable, the winds carrying secrets to them. But the only known Wind Walker had recently been killed in a war he didn't care about. It was yet to be seen if her daughter would be blessed with the gift.

"Lower your hood," the prince said.

"I'd rather not," Rayner returned, and the prince's brow arched.

"Do you know who I am?"

"Of course I know who you are."

The smirk became a full grin now. "Good. Then a formal introduction on my end is unnecessary." When Rayner said nothing, he pressed, "Am I to simply call you what you are then, or will you deign to share your name?"

"What do you think I am?"

The Fire Prince leaned in closer, his voice dropping low. "I think you are someone who sees and hears everything, yet is never seen himself," he answered, echoing Rayner's thoughts from moments ago. "I have been trying to find you for over a decade."

"I think you have mistaken me for someone else, your Highness."

"Sorin," he said. "Call me Sorin, and I am certain I have not mistaken anything. I rarely make such errors."

Arrogant prick.

Silence fell among them as the barkeep arrived again, placing a mug down in front of the female. He also placed a glass of amber liquor in front of Sorin. When Sorin held out more coin to the male to cover the drinks, the barkeep tried to decline. He said the drinks were on the house, but Sorin insisted, shoving far more coin than required into the male's hand.

Rayner watched the exchange curiously. The female's grey eyes flicked to the prince for a moment before she picked up her mug and took a deep drink without a word of gratitude. The prince didn't seem to care. His attention already settled back on Rayner. He seemed to sense Rayner's question despite not being able to see his face.

"I would introduce her to you, but it seems unfair for you to know both our names when we do not know yours," Sorin said.

"She is your consort then?" Rayner asked.

The female spluttered, choking on the drink she'd just taken.

Sorin looked at her with amusement as she continued to cough around the ale she'd undoubtedly swallowed wrong. "No. She is not my consort. She is a sentry in my armies with a foul-temper who gets into all sorts of trouble if she is not watched over."

Red splotches appeared on the female's cheeks. Not embarrassment, but fury. Rayner would recognize that type of rage on anyone. Honestly, he had to commend her for holding her tongue. He had a feeling it was only because she didn't wish to disrespect the prince in a public setting. She didn't strike him as someone who would care about offending him otherwise. But he'd watched enough people from the ashes over the decades to recognize that something was fractured in the female. That she may be harsh and ill-tempered, but she was also barely hanging on. Somehow the prince was helping her keep it all together, not as a consort as he stated, but as…something.

Something he'd never had before. What would it be like to simply have people in your life who didn't want something from you?

Didn't matter. He didn't need others. They got in the way of what he needed to do.

"I have a problem," Sorin said.

There it was. Back to being sought out because someone wanted something from him. The prince probably desired help in this war that had been playing out for centuries. Rayner knew the prince's parents had been killed by Queen Esmeray a few years ago, but Rayner had been unconcerned with the war. He had his own war to wage. The people of this continent could fight and kill each other all they wanted. He had other things to hunt down and kill.

"You are the Fire Prince with multiple resources at your disposal," Rayner answered.

"Yes, but they are all proving to be ineffective."

"I do not care about this war."

Sorin waved a dismissive hand. "We are all breathing easier since Queen Eliné and Queen Henna put up the wards to keep out those who wish our people harm. Plus, I have other people at my disposal for that, as you said. They are quite effective at their jobs. My people wish to return to their normal lives after decades of war."

Rayner still didn't care, but he was rather intrigued at this point. When he didn't respond, Sorin took it as a sign to continue with his request.

"There is a thief in my Court. One that has proven even harder to track down than you. I have been receiving complaints of large amounts of coin and other valuables mysteriously going missing."

Rayner scoffed. "I am sure the wealthy will survive the loss of a little coin."

"Yes, but while the thief does seem to target the elite, they do not appear to discriminate either. Only the poorest of my Court seem to be left alone from what we can tell over the decades."

"*Decades?*" Rayner repeated.

Sorin nodded, face going serious. Gone was the slight smirk and arrogance. In its place was what one would expect the Fire Prince to look like. Embers flickered in his golden irises at the fury he felt on behalf of his people. This was a prince who did whatever was required of him to fight for those in his charge.

"Yes," Sorin answered. "As I said, our efforts have proven fruitless. The thief does not seem to have any pattern. One report comes in from Threlarion, the next from a village nestled in the Fiera Mountains. Then one comes in from Solembra, with the next near the mortal border."

"The port city as well, I am assuming?" Rayner asked.

"Oddly, no. Aelyndee is the one place no one has reported any theft. There is theft there, of course, but from what we can tell, it is not this particular thief."

That was odd. One would think the docks full of goods would be a prime location for such thieving.

"I would pay you for your time and expertise, of course," Sorin continued. "Whatever resources I have would be at your disposal."

"I appreciate the offer, but I have my own matters to tend to," Rayner said, reaching for his mug.

"Anything I can offer assistance with?"

Rayner blinked at the prince, not that he could see him with his hood still in place. "What?"

"These tasks you have. Can I be of assistance in any way?"

"I do not exchange favors or work."

"Understood. I am not offering under such assumptions. I would offer my assistance even if I was not seeking your help," Sorin answered, sipping at his liquor.

That…didn't seem right. No one simply offered services without expecting something in return. Not that the prince could help anyway. No one could help him with this task. You had to carry the brand to find the entrance to the cliffs, and then there was navigating the various levels.

"Again, I appreciate the offer, but I do not think there is much you can do to assist me."

The prince's brows rose. "You understand I am the sitting Royal? I have numerous resources at my disposal. Relations with other Courts. Relations with other territories, including the Shifters."

"As I said, I do not think there is much you can do to assist me."

Sorin sat back in his chair, his golden stare intense as he tried to peer beneath the hood. "What will it take to convince you to aid me in this matter?"

"Respectfully, I decline any and all offers."

The female huffed a snort of amusement, and Sorin sent her a look that said he was not impressed. He sat in silence for a few moments, appearing to be debating something internally, before he said, "Whenever you complete your tasks, find me. I trust you will be able to track me down. And if you find you could use my assistance after all with those tasks… Well, again, you know how to find me." Sorin stood, tossing a purse of coin onto the table. "Consider it an advance if you decide to take me up on my offer, and if not…" He shrugged. "Consider it compensation for your time today."

"I don't need it," Rayner said, trying to shove the coin purse back at him, but Sorin was already stepping away from the table, the female moving with him.

Sorin shrugged again, looking back over his shoulder. "Then give it to someone who does, Ash Rider."

"Rayner," he called after him when he'd taken a few more steps, unsure why he was suddenly offering up his name. "My name is Rayner."

Sorin looked back again and nodded, the arrogant smirk ghosting over his lips once more. He turned back to the female, and Rayner heard him say, "I will get you a portal back to the palace. I have to meet with Eliné."

The Fae Queen.

How had Rayner forgotten that the Fire Prince was also the Fae Queen's Second?

The Fae Queen was powerful, and rumor had it, she had access to some ancient magic. Power that had long ago disappeared from this world.

Rayner lurched to his feet as he called, "Fire Prince."

Sorin turned once more, a brow raised in question.

"Perhaps there is something you can assist me with after all."

CHAPTER 5

"Sorin!"

A youngling's voice pierced the silence as Sorin escorted Rayner through the Black Halls. His hood was down. The guards of the Halls had refused him entry unless he revealed his face, and Rayner needed the help of the Fae Queen more than he needed to remain unseen, so he'd complied.

He paused when Sorin stopped outside of what appeared to be a sitting room, and a child of no more than three was making her way as fast as she could on little legs to the prince. Tangled mahogany hair surrounded her small face, and her jade green eyes were full of delight and fixed entirely on Sorin.

The Fire Prince crouched down, catching her gently. "Talwyn, what are you doing awake?" He glanced up at the harried nursemaid, who was making her way over. "Should she not be napping?"

"Tell her that," the nursemaid replied, blowing stray hair from her face.

The child just giggled.

Talwyn Semiria. Orphaned daughter of the late Queen Henna, Queen Eliné's sister. The child would be the Fae Queen of the Eastern

Courts when she was of age. Until then, it appeared her aunt was raising her.

"I will watch her for a bit, Rosemary. Take a break," Sorin said, still crouched before the Fae Princess who was peering up at Rayner. She watched him, eyes narrowed in suspicion as she pressed into Sorin.

The nursemaid wrung her fingers together. "Are you sure, your Highness? I do not wish to impose."

"It is fine, Rosemary," Sorin answered, a warm smile filling his face. "Do whatever you need to do."

The nursemaid bowed, excusing herself, and Rayner's attention was drawn back to the prince when Talwyn said, "Fire, Sorin!"

The prince chuckled, flames springing up and moving around the room while the princess chased them about. Sorin pushed back to his feet, lifting a hand, and a fire message disappeared among some flames. "I will have Eliné meet us here."

Rayner merely nodded, unable to tear his eyes away from the little girl. Memories of another child with bright red hair giggling while his ashes had drifted around her and she tried to catch them in her small hands.

"Rayner?"

He blinked, finding the Fire Prince studying him. Rayner cleared his throat, forcing himself to look away from Talwyn. "Yes?"

The prince appeared to hesitate before he said, "I want to make it clear that I do not expect any form of repayment for arranging this audience. You are not indebted to me in any way."

Rayner stared back at him. "You want nothing?"

"I still hope you will reconsider and aid me, but I am not requiring such a thing."

"Sorin?"

They both turned at the sound of the feminine voice, and Rayner took in the Fae Queen. She was ethereal. Dark brown hair was swept into a knot at her nape, icy blue eyes surveying them all. A silver circlet sat atop her brow, and she smiled when her gaze landed on her niece.

"Eliné," Sorin said, striding towards her. "This is Rayner."

"Your Majesty," Rayner greeted, bowing at the waist.

"A pleasure, Rayner," she replied. Her head tilted as he straightened. "Sorin has been searching for you for quite some time."

"This has nothing to do with that," Sorin cut in quickly, catching Talwyn by the arm when she tripped over the rug and nearly landed on her face. The child giggled as he swung her up, settling her on his shoulders. "I will leave you two to visit while I take this one to nap."

"No!" Talwyn cried, squirming atop his shoulders, but then she was giggling again as tiny flames danced along her arms and feet.

Eliné watched them leave. She waited a bit before she said to the two sentries standing guard. "Leave us." The pair hesitated, but when the queen sent them another look, they bowed their heads before doing as they'd been ordered. When the doors to the room were shut, she motioned to a set of armchairs near the hearth. "Please sit."

"After you, your Majesty," Rayner replied, stepping back for her to pass.

When they were both seated, Eliné's hands folded and resting in her lap, she said, "What can I do for you, Rayner?"

It was strange to hear his name. So few knew it, and even fewer used it. It was always Ash Rider. Known for what he could do, not for who he was.

"I am in need of your knowledge."

A brow arched. "I am intrigued."

"Do you know of a way to kill a being who can manipulate and control emotion?"

Eliné went utterly still. "There are no such beings in this world."

"But if there were, how would you defeat one? Shirastone does not seem to affect—"

"You speak as if there is one in this world, Rayner," the queen interrupted, the temperature in the room dropping noticeably.

"There is," he confirmed. "She is powerful, and I do not believe her to be Fae, but something…else."

The Fae Queen stood abruptly. "Where? Where is this being?"

"The Southern Islands," Rayner answered, watching her begin to pace in front of the hearth.

"There is nothing on those islands."

"There is an entire colony hidden among some cliffs. There are powerful enchantments around them."

"Who? Tell me her name," Eliné demanded.

"Those forced to live there call her the Baroness, but her name is Moranna."

Eliné hissed a soft curse at the name. She was muttering, speaking to herself, and the only thing Rayner could catch was, "She must have come through with…" She cut herself off, turning and offering Rayner an apologetic smile. "Forgive me. It has been a very long time since I have heard that name."

"You know her?"

"I know of her. I know…" Eliné grimaced, her icy blue eyes holding pity when she met Rayner's gaze. "I know what she does. I know how you likely came into this world. I did not know she was here though, or I swear to Saylah, I would have done something. I will take care of this."

But Rayner was already shaking his head. "Her death is mine."

He proceeded to tell the Fae Queen what he knew, how he had been Moranna's personal guard, how he had learned what she was doing, the curse that took his memories, and what he had been doing since the Oracle had helped him recover them. He left out the parts about Breya and Aravis. She might be willing to help him, but he didn't trust anyone with information like that. Not when it could easily be used against him. Not when Aravis was still being used against him.

The queen clasped her hands behind her back. "You are correct in your belief that she is not Fae. She was created to serve a different purpose. Shirastone does not affect her because she is not Fae."

"She has bands of deathstone. Not much, but she has these bands for the wrists that stifle my gifts. Do you know of a way to combat that?"

Eliné shook her head. "There is no way to combat deathstone, and such a thing would suppress her gifts, but then you are still with the problem of actually ending her."

"There are also wards around the islands," Rayner continued. "They used to just be around the cliffs themselves, but I was informed on my last visit that she has somehow warded the entirety of the islands. She knows the moment I step onto them, so taking her by surprise will not be an option."

The queen smoothed her hands down her dress. "If you have some time, I may have a few things that can be of assistance. I can have food prepared for you?"

"I am fine, thank you."

She nodded. "Would you like a room to rest?"

"I am fine here if that is all right with you."

She nodded again. "I will send some refreshments."

Rayner could have told her it wasn't necessary, but he knew she'd do so anyway. Royal propriety and all that.

It was perhaps ten minutes later when the doors to the small sitting room opened again. It wasn't the help with refreshments though, and it wasn't the Fae Queen. It was the Fire Prince, a sleeping princess in his arms, head resting on his shoulder. There was some sort of chocolate smeared on her cheek.

"Eliné said you were staying for a bit," Sorin said by way of greeting. Rayner only nodded, eyes fixed on the sleeping child. "I would take her to her room, but I promised to be here when she woke up. I don't break my promises to her."

Rayner nodded again. He'd made promises too.

And then broken them.

"But I can keep you company," Sorin added after a stint of silence.

"That's not necessary."

"I know," Sorin replied, gently laying the sleeping princess on a sofa and covering her with a blanket. "Not necessary, but I also told Eliné I would deliver these."

There was a burst of flame along a small table and a tray of sandwiches, nuts, cheese, and drinks appeared.

"Also not necessary," Rayner said.

Sorin shrugged, moving towards the food. "Eat or don't. I will keep you company either way."

Rayner watched him fill a plate. Then watched him float that plate over to him on a flame along with a glass of liquor before he started fixing another plate for himself. But Rayner could just stand there, holding the plate and glass. When Sorin turned back to him, he stopped mid-step, a brow lifting in question.

"You are serving me?" Rayner asked.

"Do you need to get your own food?"

"You are a prince."

"Whose job is to serve those in his care. Do you not have a residence in Solembra?"

"Yes, but—"

Sorin grinned, jerking his chin toward an armchair. "Just take a seat and eat, Rayner."

He waited until Sorin had taken a seat in the armchair the queen had sat in before he lowered into the one opposite him. Sorin already had half a sandwich gone when Rayner said, "Thank you again for arranging an audience with the queen."

Sorin waved him off. "What do you plan to do when you have accomplished these tasks of yours?"

Rayner blinked at him, the plate forgotten in his lap. "I've never thought about it."

"You have family?" He glanced at the sleeping princess. "Children?"

"No," Rayner answered. "No children."

"Family then." Rayner stared back at him. "I am not trying to pry," Sorin said, setting his plate off to the side. "My parents were

killed a few years ago. This war is finally dying down with the wards up
to keep my people safe. We are…rebuilding."

As terrible as it was, Rayner felt himself relax at the prince
speaking of his own loss and keeping the focus on himself. He picked
up a sandwich, listening to the Fire Prince speak of his Court, plans he
had for the future, relations with the other Courts and territories, and
Rayner found himself asking follow-up questions. Not because he
cared per se, but because…

Because he'd never actually had casual conversation with someone
like this. His gifts had emerged when he was twelve, and he'd immediately been sequestered away. He'd been trained by private tutors in all
areas—his studies, combat, magic—and once he'd mastered them all,
he'd been assigned as Moranna's personal guard. No one wanted to be
associated with the Baroness's personal guard. He had been hers, just
as she'd always wanted.

He'd always been alone. He'd never considered the idea that he
didn't have to be. That once Moranna was dead and those islands were
nothing but a graveyard, it didn't have to be just him and Aravis.

So when the Fae Queen returned, requesting to speak with Rayner
privately, he stood while Sorin gathered the still slumbering Talwyn. "I
have connections across the continent and throughout your Court. I
will have them start looking for this thief, and when my tasks are
complete, I will find you."

"That is not necessary," Sorin replied. "As I said, you are under no
obligation to repay me for anything."

"I understand, but I will still have them look into it. They might
already know something the way it is."

Sorin nodded. "I appreciate it."

When he had left, the doors being closed behind him, he found
himself once again alone with the Fae Queen. She lifted a hand, and a
dagger appeared amidst a flurry of snow. It wasn't anything special.
The blade wasn't even shirastone. It was just…a dagger. Fiera steel
maybe? But Rayner knew that would not be enough for Moranna.

He was trying to figure out a way to word his refusal of the weapon without sounding like a complete ass, when the ghost of a smile flitted across the queen's lips. "I know it does not appear to be anything special, but since your gifts will most likely be inaccessible when you face her, you shall need something to fight with." She held the dagger out to him, and he took it, turning it over in his hands, trying to see if he'd missed something. "It is imbued with magic not found on this continent," she continued.

"Then how will I access it?" Rayner asked. It wasn't uncommon for weapons to be imbued, but the bearer needed to possess that same power to access the magic.

"With ancient magic that has long been lost to this land," the Fae Queen answered. Another flurry of snowflakes, and a book appeared in her hand. It was an old book, leather and worn, and when she opened the cover, it was a language he could not read. She flipped to a particular page before turning the book around and holding it out to show him. On the page was a Mark, but nothing like the Fae Marks that were given by the Artists. This one was sharper, harsher somehow.

"This is Blood Magic," Rayner finally said.

The queen smiled softly. "That is one name for it, yes."

"I cannot perform Blood Magic."

"The Ash Rider gifts are rare gifts from Anala, Rayner," she answered gently. "I think you will find there are still secrets to be discovered about what those gifts can offer you."

"You speak like an Oracle," he mumbled before silently chastising himself for the insolence.

She just laughed softly. "While I do possess Witch gifts as my sister possessed Shifter gifts, my gifts of prophecy are quite lacking, I am afraid." The humor slipped from her features a moment later. "Moranna, however, was in service to a very powerful being who taught her many things. Moranna may not be a Witch, but many of their spells and ways can be learned without such gifts. It simply takes more effort and sacrifice. This Mark will activate the magic imbued in the dagger. The first Water Prince imbued it at the Eternal Springs when Fae first came to these lands. Study the Mark. Memorize it. I cannot let you take this book, but beware, Rayner. If that Mark is not done perfectly, things will not end well for you."

"What is the cost?"

He wasn't a fool. All magic had a cost, and Blood Magic required the greatest sacrifices of all.

"The magic contained in that dagger could very well take your life when it takes hers," Eliné answered.

That was fine. As long as Aravis got out, he would gladly give his own life if it meant taking Moranna from this world. He could speak with the Fire Prince. After spending only a few hours with the male, Rayner could tell the prince would do whatever he could to help him, including helping Aravis get settled into his home. Rayner would leave everything to her. He already had. A will was secured at the bank with instructions for all his assets to go to her upon his death.

But if he did survive this…

He met the queen's stare. "There is one other thing I was hoping you would aid me with."

CHAPTER 6

"Fuck," Rayner muttered when his boot slipped on the cliff side. The spray from the waves crashing on the rocks below made the surface extra slick, and the grips on his boots were doing absolutely nothing to help. He already had a particularly nasty gash along his brow from an earlier slide down the rocky side.

Gritting his teeth, he regained his footing and pulled himself up, his fingertips digging into the ledge he was holding onto. He'd always used his gifts to find his way into the cliffs, to find that weakness in the wards, but he was conserving every drop of his magic tonight. Moranna knew he was here with that enchantment she had around the islands, but she never seemed to tell anyone when he would come to wreak havoc. The guards were never on high alert. He'd surprised Feris in his godsdamn rooms. He was banking on her not telling them he was here this time either, and he didn't want to run into any of them. Which was nearly impossible without his magic since he'd need to go through the hidden entrance.

Which was why he was climbing the fucking cliffs.

Because near the top, there was a ledge that served as a balcony for Moranna's rooms. The ledge was small. Just enough room for a small table and two chairs. The ledge itself was sunk into the cliff side and not visible from the outside. It was her other failsafe. When he had resided here, he was fairly certain he was the only one who knew about it. He didn't know if that was still the case or not, but it was his only way in without using any magic.

He was hoping once he made it up there, he would have some time to try to figure out where the entrance was to this secret passageway she'd used the night she'd killed Breya in front of him. From what he could piece together, she had more secret rooms where she was keeping Aravis and the most powerful. If she was in her rooms, he'd deal with it, but he was hoping it was early enough in the night she wouldn't have retired yet. If her habits hadn't changed over the decades though, she wouldn't come to bed until well after midnight.

The dagger the Fae Queen had given him was strapped to his belt beneath his cloak. He had shirastone knives down his boots, and twin short swords strapped to his back with Fiera steel. He still had that arrow with a deathstone tip stored in a pocket realm too, but if his magic was inaccessible, he wouldn't be able to get to it.

He heaved himself up onto the ledge, staying in a crouch as he surveyed the space. The moonlight couldn't even reach into the dark space of the alcove. There was no railing, nothing that would make a passing ship think something was up here.

Rayner moved silently into the shadows, stepping around the table and chairs and pushing open the glass doors. He felt the wards ripple around him. He didn't know if Moranna was able to tell exactly where he was, but either way, he didn't want to waste time. Pulling his hood down, he took in the rooms. Nothing had really changed. A sofa in front of the hearth. A large walk-in dressing room and attached bathing room. A small dining set. A large bed off to one side.

The male in it though.

That was new, considering that had once been him.

If he was her new personal guard, he was shit at it. The male hadn't even stirred when he'd entered. Rayner didn't have time to play tonight though. He gathered smoke from the fire in the hearth and sent it straight into the male's lungs, overwhelming him before his Fae instincts could try to counteract it and heal him.

When he could no longer hear the male's heart beating, he shifted his attention back to the rest of the room. He took in the walls, how furniture was arranged, where decor was placed. Anything that would give him some type of clue as to where the entrance to this secret passageway was. When he came up with nothing, he released his ashes, letting them feel along the cracks and divots in the stone.

He was about to give up when the ashes called him into her dressing room. He followed their path, black and white dust fluttering to the floor, guiding him behind a section of red gowns that he shoved to the side. There was nothing remarkable behind them. The wall was pristine white stone. No grooves or cracks or indents.

He swiped his hand down his face in frustration before he ran his palm along the smooth expanse, searching for a trigger of some sort, startled when he left a smear of blood in his wake. The wound above his brow, he realized. He was keeping a tight leash on his magic, which included his ability to heal himself. But the smeared blood was flaring slightly, appearing to glow, and then an archway was appearing. Just like the main entrance that appeared in the presence of the brand beneath his skin.

Stone steps descended, torches lining the walls every few feet. These walls were not the white of the colony though. They were brown and weathered, like the outside of the cliffs. Pulling his hood back up over his head, he stepped inside, making his way down. It was nearly five minutes before he reached a passageway that branched off from the still descending stairs, and Rayner took it, not wanting to overlook anything.

There were wooden doors lining the passageway, all of them containing small windows with shirastone bars across them. When he peered in a few, he found basic living quarters. Beds, sofas, hearths. They appeared to have bathing rooms attached as well. Some were empty while some rooms also contained sleeping Fae who all appeared healthy and well-nourished. He wondered if their eyes would look as haunted and dead as so many of the others in the colony looked if they were awake.

He kept going, checking each room for signs of Aravis, but when he reached the end, he hadn't found her. So he trudged back, descending the stairs once more. It was ten minutes before he reached another passageway. There were wooden doors down this one too, but they were far more interspersed. There were no windows on these doors either. He checked every one of them. One appeared to be a records room. Rows and rows of shelves stacked with papers. Another was a small library with books lining the walls. He continued along, finding more of the same, until he came to a room at the end of the passageway.

This one had double doors, and they weren't wood like the rest of them had been. These doors were heavy stone, intricate carvings etched into them. He traced his finger along one of them, realizing they weren't symbols at all but a language. The wards were stronger around this room, and he loosed some ashes to find their way in, seeking out the weak spots. It took longer than he expected, and it took far more of his magic than he liked to work out a point past them. But he found it. A hairline crack near the center, just enough for him to get through in his smoke.

He materialized on the other side of the doors, finding himself inside a large room. There were various tables throughout. Some had cauldrons smoking atop them. Others had papers and books strewn about. There were some with herbs and plants. There were five different hearths, all lit.

An apothecary room, Rayner realized. This was a large apothecary room like the Witches had. Eliné had said Moranna had been extensively trained by a powerful being who had taught her the way around spells and blood magic. He was looking at the proof of that.

He took a few careful steps into the room, not wanting to upset any of the potions brewing or elixirs cooling. Activating even one of them could alter all of his plans. He made his way over to some of the notes, muttering a curse when he again found them all written in a language he could not read. The books were the same.

His gifts were buzzing beneath his skin, and he let his ashes out, if only to release some tension. They speared across the room to a bookcase, and Rayner followed. A few of the shelves held books. A couple of them held various instruments and scales, but on the middle shelf was something else. On one side sat a replica of what he could only assume were various worlds that were thought to exist. Which one was their own, he couldn't say, but beside the replica sat another sphere off by itself. This one had symbols too, but they differed from anything he had ever seen. The symbols seemed to move, fading in and out in a way that held him captive. He didn't realize what he was doing when he lifted a hand, reaching for the thing, too mesmerized by it to note his own actions.

The tip of his finger skimmed over it, all the symbols fading away so it was nothing but a light grey orb. He called some ashes forth, letting them drift around it, but the symbols did not return. Nothing happened at all.

He let his hand fall to his side at the same time a female voice said from behind him, "How incredibly disappointing."

He spun, finding Moranna standing in the doorway. Red dress. Black hair with red streaks pinned back. Dark eyes. Red painted lips. Exactly as she had looked the day she'd sent him from these very walls.

"Moranna," Rayner said, his tone dark and cold.

She stepped into the room, graceful and fluid as ever, moving to a table. She stirred a cauldron, sprinkling crushed herbs into it. "I see you have finally returned home with purpose."

"I have had purpose every time I have returned to these wretched islands," Rayner spat, calculating her every movement.

"I have let you come back here. Let you get this vengeance you seem to need. I have not interfered once, but last time, my Ash

Rider…" She trailed off, moving to another table. "Last time you made a very unwise choice in regards to whom you took from me."

"Feris was always going to die. Just as the rest of them will. It was only a matter of time," Rayner retorted.

"Feris is not of whom I speak," Moranna scoffed, bracing her hands atop a worktable and leveling him with a cold glare. "One of my most powerful vessels disappeared that day. I can only assume it was you."

"I took no one out with me that day," he countered. He still hadn't moved, still trying to figure out his best course of action. He'd scarcely killed anyone the last time he had come here. Three overseers and Feris. That had been it.

"I let you go out into the world," Moranna continued. "I let you wander the continent, learn what you thought you needed, and waited for you to come back with all that knowledge. And you repay me in this way?"

"I was always coming back to kill you, Moranna."

She laughed. "You cannot kill me, Rayner. You know if you do, your beloved sister dies."

"Where is Aravis?"

Moranna held up her hand, a band of deathstone held between her fingers. "Put this on, and I will take you to her. Then we will discuss what must be done in regards to your poor choices."

"And if I refuse?"

She smiled at him, the kind that told him she was humoring him. "You will never find her."

Rayner stalked forward, snatching the band and sliding it onto his wrist. His ashes thrashed beneath his skin, unable to break through, before they eventually quieted into nothing. Moranna reached up, patting his cheek. "Wise choice, my Ash Rider."

"I will kill you before the sun rises," Rayner gritted out.

"You are powerful, Rayner, but not that powerful. Come."

He fell into step beside her, grimacing internally at how natural this felt. How he had done this thousands of times. Escorted her all over the cliffs, but never here. Never to this secret place within the secret colony. How many did she keep here? And if he was one of the most powerful, why hadn't she kept *him* here?

Moranna led him back down the passageway to the stairs where they descended to the next passageway. The Baroness stopped outside a room, her hand on the handle. "Remember that her survival depends on you."

It always had. That's why he was here.

And tonight he would ensure her survival was no longer in the hands of Moranna.

Moranna pushed the door open, stepping aside so Rayner could enter, and there she was. Sitting near a hearth, doing needlework. Healthy and whole. Raven black hair braided into a plait hung over her shoulder as she focused on her task.

And then she looked up.

Rayner sucked in a breath when grey eyes that matched his own without the swirling landed on him. They were haunted and broken like so many others he had seen, but there was also something in them he never glimpsed in the others.

Hope. There was a glimmer of hope there.

She dropped her needlework, lurching to her feet, a hand coming to her chest. Rayner reached up, pulling back his hood so she could see his face.

"Rayner?" she whispered, but he could only nod. Her eyes flicked over his shoulder before settling back on him. "What have you done?"

"Now you have seen her. Alive and well. Let's discuss the terms for keeping her that way," Moranna said softly from behind him.

The sound of her voice—the way she spoke to him about Aravis— had the monster she'd created waking deep in his soul. Rayner descended to that place where the Reaper dwelled inside him. Aravis must have noticed the shift because her eyes widened slightly, and she took a step back from him as he turned to face the Baroness.

"What are your terms?"

"You remain here, where you belong," Moranna said. "I have let you roam long enough, and you have taken much from me. Too much. I was hoping when you returned you would have learned more about your gifts, but it appears even that was a waste."

"You wish for me to return to being your personal guard?" Rayner asked. "Just go back to how things were?"

"Oh no," Moranna purred, stepping up to him. Her hand came up, brushing back hair from his brow. "You see, your sister has been unable to produce any offspring of quality. But I suspect you might, with all that ash and smoke running through your veins. There are a few bloodlines I wish to cross with yours. I was hoping the blood you supplied me when you left would be enough, but it has not been. None of it has been enough." She trailed off, muttering more to herself by the end.

"If I agree to this, no one touches Aravis again. *No one*," Rayner said. "I am given free access to her and her to me."

"You will return to my bed, like before," Moranna countered. "But I agree to allow you to visit her whenever your duties allow you to do so."

"And no one else will touch her," Rayner repeated. "I want a Blood Vow, Moranna."

Aravis sucked in a breath, at the demand for a Blood Vow or the use of Moranna's name, he wasn't sure. Moranna's lips tilted up in a victorious grin. "Of course."

He pulled a dagger from his belt. An unremarkable blade of Fiera steel. He sliced it across his palm, the deathstone stifling his healing abilities. Moranna held out her own hand, her smile growing when he sliced along her palm next.

"I agree to your terms of aiding you in producing powerful offspring."

"Rayner, no!" Aravis cried, lurching forward, but Moranna held up a hand. Aravis immediately stilled, her features filling with horror as she watched.

"I will resume my role as your personal guard, in whatever capacity you require of me," Rayner continued. "All these things I vow to uphold for as long as you remain on this side of the Veil. I vow and swear this with my blood."

"I agree to your terms that no one touches Aravis again. She will remain here and be given free access to you, but she will not be required to perform her duties any longer," Moranna said. "I vow and swear this with my blood."

Their palms met, and when Rayner glanced at Aravis, he saw silent tears tracking down her face. She was shaking her head in disbelief, but Rayner had sworn long ago he would do whatever was necessary to keep her safe. To keep them both safe. He'd failed Breya. He would not fail Aravis.

"Welcome home, my Ash Rider," Moranna said, intertwining the fingers of their still joined palms. "Let's go celebrate your return." She tugged on his hand, leading him to the door. He only had a moment to look back over his shoulder at Aravis.

The hope he'd glimpsed in her eyes was gone.

CHAPTER 7

He let Moranna lead him back up the stones of the secret passageways to her quarters at the top of the cliffs. The archway dissolved back into the wall in her dressing room when they emerged.

"I'm going to clean up," she said, finally releasing his hand. Her palm had already healed. His was still steadily bleeding. She frowned slightly, fingers brushing over the band on his wrist. "You understand why I cannot remove this yet, yes?"

"Of course, your Grace," he replied, stepping aside to let her pass.

Her frown morphed into a smile, and she sighed wistfully. "How I have missed you. Your replacements have been…inadequate."

He smiled faintly, nodding his head, and she moved out to the bathing room. He followed, slipping beyond into the bedroom where he removed his cloak, boots, and various weapons.

For Aravis. This was all for her. He didn't matter as long as she was safe.

He was pulling his tunic over his head when Moranna stepped from the bathing room wearing nothing but a sheer red robe. Her dark hair spilled over her shoulders, hunger shining in her eyes as they raked over him. She held out a hand to him, and when he took it, she tugged him over to the bed. She shoved at his chest, pushing him down onto the mattress, and he went willingly. Anything required of him to keep Aravis from being touched like this again.

Moranna climbed into his lap, fingers sinking into his hair while she straddled his waist, her breasts pressing against his chest. "So many travels," she murmured. "Yet you keep coming back." She brushed her lips across his. "You have always been mine. No matter how far you strayed."

He gripped her hips, tugging her closer, and she gasped lightly at the movement. He slid a hand up her spine before grasping the back of her neck.

"When you have proven yourself loyal to me once more, I can remove that band," she said. "Then I can see all that power swirling in your eyes."

"Whatever you desire, your Grace," he replied, bringing her mouth to his. She deepened the kiss instantly, hunger and lust and want driving her. He opened when she nipped at his bottom lip, meeting each stroke of her tongue with his own. Her hands were roaming over him, down his arms, across her chest. Fingers skated along his torso, and when they reached for the ties on his pants, he flipped them.

Another gasp came from her when he settled between her thighs, her robe falling open. He broke their kiss, bracing himself on one hand while he trailed his fingertips up her abdomen, between the valley of her breasts. She squirmed beneath him, and he could sense her growing impatience.

"I learned some fascinating tricks on my travels," he murmured, fingers moving along her collarbone.

"Do tell," she said breathlessly, hips pressing up against him. "Or better yet, show me."

The corner of his lips tipped up. "I plan to, your Grace." His fingers trailed downwards again, stopping over her heart. He pressed his palm flat, leaving a smear of blood from his still bleeding palm.

"This reunion is all about you," he went on, fingers trailing around one breast, then the other. "It has always been about you." They trailed back up the valley of her breasts, into the blood smear. "But now that I am bound irrevocably to you, tell me, your Grace. What are we working so hard to achieve?"

She smiled up at him, eyes brightening with a different kind of hunger. "Power, my Ash Rider," she breathed, her back arching as his finger kept moving. The lightest of touches to keep her seeking more, keep her on the edge of anticipation. "The more power I can breed for my king, the more power he will bestow upon me. And now that you are back where you belong, I can finally make progress. I am hoping that one of your offspring will be able to activate the—"

But her words got stuck in her throat, her eyes flying wide.

A wicked smile filled Rayner's face as he leaned in close, the dagger piercing her chest sliding in a little further. "I do not give a single fuck," he whispered.

"You cannot kill me," she rasped, fingers clawing at his hand that was holding the blade in place. "You are not powerful enough. No one here is."

"I am aware," he replied. "Which is why I sought help. From a Fae Queen. She seemed to know of you."

Moranna's lip curled up into a sneer despite the agony. "Eliné," she hissed. "In service to the daughter of the traitorous ones. I told Alaric to take care of her." She grimaced when Rayner twisted the dagger. "But even she is not powerful enough. Fae magic cannot take my life. As much as this hurts, it is nothing compared to what your punishment will be for this poor choice," she gasped. She coughed then, blood trickling from the corner of her mouth.

"I know that too," Rayner answered, reaching with his other hand to swipe up the blood with his fingertip. He began drawing a Mark on her chest.

Right above the Blood Mark he'd stabbed the dagger into. In a moment, he would place the final line of that Mark and trigger whatever magic was in the dagger. It might take his life, it might not. But in the off chance he survived…

"What are you doing?" Moranna gasped, struggling even more beneath him.

"I want this enchantment you have around these islands," he replied, continuing the Mark. "When you are gone from this world, living your eternity in the Pits of Torment, I want these islands to die with you. No one will inhabit them ever again. I want to know if someone sets foot on them."

She laughed, and it turned into another cough, more blood sliding down her chin. "My sweet, naïve, Ash Rider. Not only is your sister bound here by these wards, you can only transfer this enchantment with Blood Magic, and there is only one being who has created such a Mark."

"Then this one shouldn't affect you," Rayner said, his manic grin growing when Moranna went still beneath him. "I think you already know I can use the Marks though, and once I control the enchantments, I can let Aravis leave them."

"Rayner, wait," she gasped. "Wait, you don't know everything. Let me explain—"

But she was arching off the bed again when he completed the Mark, the dagger sinking deeper into her chest. He felt it. The shift. Something settling over him, and then he could *feel* the islands themselves. Every soul moving among them. Those in the cliffs. The merchants at the docks. All of them.

"You are going to regret that," Moranna snarled.

Rayner said nothing. Just lifted his hand, showing her his still bleeding palm. "The Fae Queen also gave me this dagger. Said it was imbued by the first Water Prince at the Eternal Springs."

Her thrashing turned frantic, hands clawing at him. "Please, Rayner. Whatever you like, it is yours. You want to leave? Go! You want to take Aravis with you? It is done!"

He bent over her once more, the dagger sliding in to the hilt. "The only thing I want, *your Grace*, is for your death to be as painful as possible. The Fae Queen assured me that would be the case."

He moved to bring his hand down, but her nails raked down his arm, drawing more blood. He tried to brush her hand aside, but she dug her nails in further. With a final yank, he pulled free, grasping the dagger with his bleeding hand.

But not before her fingers hooked on the deathstone band in her desperate attempts to stop him. The band slid off, being flung through the air at the same time that black flames flared out from the dagger. Rayner was thrown off of her, flying across the room by the blast of the flames. Flames that were so hot he should have been incinerated on the spot, but his ashes were pouring out of him, a tight shield forming and growing thicker as it strained to guard him from the onslaught of dark fire.

Moranna was screaming, and Rayner flipped onto his hands and knees to watch as the black flames consumed her. Eliné had promised she would suffer, and she hadn't been lying. His magic was being pushed to its limits as it held back the flames from reaching him. He knew he wouldn't be able to hold out much longer. And that was fine. He would go to his death willingly as soon as he was sure Moranna had gone there first.

Her screams died moments before his magic gave out, and when silence settled, he felt a ripple of power rush from the room. He didn't know what it was or what it meant, and he frankly didn't give a fuck.

Rayner stumbled to his feet, going to the bed to find nothing. Not even ashes. The black flames had consumed every last bit of her. The dagger was gone. Nothing left but scorched sheets and memories.

He turned back to the dressing room, getting dressed and strapping his weapons back into place before looping his cloak over his arm. He had arranged for merchant ships to be waiting offshore, waiting for his signal. All the innocents would come with him today. Any overseers and guards remaining would meet their deaths. When he left the islands today, they would be nothing but the graveyard he'd once said they would be.

But Aravis was first. He would get her to the merchant ships, then come back for the rest.

He raced down the stairs as fast as he could without tripping over his own feet. He was exhausted. He hadn't planned to use all of his magic reserves so quickly. It would take months to replenish any of it, and he felt hollow and empty without the comfort of his ashes.

He threw open the door to Aravis's room to find her curled in a ball on her bed, tears still streaming. She looked up at him, eyes rimmed in red.

"It's over." That was all he could say. He couldn't get anything else past the lump in his throat. But he took a step closer to her, and she was up and off the bed, throwing her arms around his neck. She clung to him, and he embraced her just as hard. "I am sorry it took so long," he murmured.

She just cried, her tears soaking into his tunic.

After several minutes, he gently eased her back, wrapping his cloak around her shoulders. "Are you ready to see the sun?"

She smiled—a real one—through her tears. "Yes," she whispered. "Yes, Rayner, I am ready to see the sun."

Her hand gripped tightly in his, he led her out of the secret passageway and back up to Moranna's rooms. He took her straight through, not letting her take in the space. He didn't want any more of her memories to be made here. They took a side stairwell that was only used by Moranna and her personal guard. It was so tight, they could only move single file down the stairs, designed that way for the Baroness's protection he'd once been told.

When they reached the bottom, they came out right next to the hall that would lead to the exit. He had Aravis wait while he took care of the guards at the archway. She didn't need to see that. She'd seen enough death to last lifetimes.

He could feel her trembling when they approached the archway, and he glanced down at her while they waited for it to form completely. She was decades old and had never seen the sun or the sky. She had never seen the sea or felt the breeze on her face. The entirety of her life had been lived inside these cliffs.

He wanted to watch every moment as she took this all in.

Her breath caught at the first glimpse of blue from the archway. She went to take a step forward, but he stopped her.

"Take off your shoes," he said, nodding at her feet. "Feel the sand between your toes."

She smiled up at him, the smile that hadn't left her face since he'd mentioned the sun. The smile he'd sworn he would see when he had set out to take her from here all those years ago.

Her shoes in one hand, he took her hand in the other and led her outside. He felt her suck in a deep breath as they stepped out onto the sand, and when they had moved down the beach, away from the cliffs, she stopped and tipped her face to the sky. The sun had just moved above the horizon, bathing everything in a morning glow.

He slipped one of his medallions from his pocket. He still carried them with him out of habit, and he was glad he had them today. They would give him just enough ashes to send a message to the merchant ships. He turned back to Aravis after he had sent the message off, intending to tell her what the plan was now, but—

He dropped to his knees where she was lying in the sand, staring up at the blue sky. She was pale, which was to be expected after living inside cliffs for decades, but the blood running from her ears, her nose, her mouth…

"What is wrong? What's happening?" Rayner demanded, not knowing what he was looking for to be able to help her.

She stared up at him, the smile still on her face. "I am bound here by the wards," she rasped softly, reaching for his hand.

"No," he said fiercely, squeezing her fingers. "I took the wards from her. I control them now. I say you can be free of them."

Her smile turned soft, and she lifted her other arm. A Mark stood out starkly on her forearm, just below the crook of her elbow. "When you left, she gave me this. Should you ever try to take me from here, it would kill me. It is separate from the other wards, Rayner."

"No," he growled again, gathering her into his arms. "I will take you back inside. I will find a way to break the Mark, and then—"

Her fingertips were pressing to his lips. "I knew what would happen when I stepped onto this beach, Rayner."

"You didn't say anything. You didn't—" He swallowed thickly, realizing his face was wet. Tears were coursing down his face. "Why didn't you say anything?" he rasped, wiping the blood from beneath her nose with the corner of his cloak still wrapped around her.

"Because I am tired, Rayner," she answered, eyes going back up to the sky. "I do not wish to live another day inside those cliffs."

"Just until I can find a way to counteract the Mark," he insisted. "Please, Aravis. Please don't do this. All of this has been for you. You and Breya. I couldn't save Breya. Let me save you. Please."

She cupped his cheek, grey eyes settling back on him. "I do not wish to live with these memories another day. You did save me, Rayner. You got me out. Now let me be free. Please."

Two tears slid down her cheeks, her thumb brushing along his jaw. He gathered her against his chest, pressing his face into her hair. "I'm sorry, Aravis. I'm sorry I took so long."

"You did not fail me, Rayner," she murmured. "You have saved hundreds of innocent people from terrible things. You have taken horrible people from this world. You killed the Baroness so no one else will suffer. You have not failed, Rayner."

He could hear her heart slowing, feel her breaths getting shallower.

"Please let me try, Aravis," he begged. "Let me take you back—"

But she was shaking her head. "I wish to cross the Veil where I can see the sun, Rayner. Please."

He stared down at her for the longest moment, and when he finally nodded, he felt her relax with relief. He shifted them so he could still hold her and she could still see the sky.

"Promise me something, Rayner," she said softly, squeezing his fingers.

"Anything," he answered hoarsely.

"You have done what you set out to do. You have liberated those beneath the cliffs. You have ended Moranna. You have saved me. When you have finished with those inside, let the Reaper die here with me. Only let him rise again to save your family."

"*You* are my family," Rayner answered, resting his cheek against the top of her head.

"Then promise me you will find another family. People to love as fiercely as you have loved me and Breya. Promise me that—" She paused, her entire body shuddering. He knew she only had a few breaths left. "Promise me you will move on from this nightmare."

"Some nightmares never end," he murmured through his tears.

"Yours will," she countered gently. "If you let it. Promise me you won't be alone anymore, Rayner."

"I promise, Aravis," he whispered. "I promise."

And he held his sister while she took her last breath, staring at the sunny sky with a smile on her face.

THE FIRE COURT THIRD

Six Years Later

"I don't even get the courtesy of being seen in his Highness's throne room?" the thief griped as Rayner led him down a hall at the Fiera Palace in Solembra. The thief craned his neck to peer into the formal dining room, then looked back at the door they'd stopped in front of. "Really? A fucking pantry?"

Rayner didn't say anything, letting his ashes push open the door as he shoved the thief through.

The Fire Prince was seated at a table, dealing two hands of cards. He looked up when the door opened, that arrogant grin Rayner saw so often these days appearing. "I was beginning to worry," Sorin said, dealing the last few cards. He nodded at the one empty seat. "Sit."

The thief looked over his shoulder at Rayner. "I'm to watch you two play cards?"

Rayner rolled his eyes. "He's talking to you, you dick. Just sit down." He stepped around the thief, moving to the bar that ran along the back of the room.

"That one's for you," Sorin said, pointing at a full liquor glass beside the cards he'd dealt.

The thief's golden eyes bounced back and forth between the Fire Prince and the Ash Rider. Rayner just sent him a taunting smile.

"I am not going to bite," Sorin drawled, taking a sip of his own liquor.

"No. You'll just toss me in your cells for a time," the thief bit back.

Sorin sighed. "Sit down, Cyrus. I have a proposition for you."

Cyrus's eyes narrowed. "How do you know my name?"

The prince sat back in his chair, swirling his glass, the ice clinking. "I know a lot about you. I know you grew up in my port city of Aelyndee, but have not been back there in decades. I know you have been a thief since you could walk. I know you have swindled more people than I can count. I know you have been robbing some of the wealthier of my subjects."

Cyrus opened his mouth to speak, but Sorin held up his hand. Rayner took a sip from his glass to hide his smirk.

He'd been working for Sorin since he came back from the islands six years ago. The prince and Eliné had helped find homes for all the innocent people he'd freed from the colony. In fact, the Water and Fire Princes had been waiting for them when they docked in the Water Court. Once they had all been settled, Rayner had taken the time he'd needed to refill his magic reserves, but he'd kept his word. He'd had people looking into this thief Sorin was having troubles with. They had quite a few leads for him to follow, and as soon as his reserves were full several months later, he'd started looking into all of them. They'd eventually led him to Cyrus, where he'd watched him single-handedly pickpocket an entire tavern in minutes and then walk into a wealthy district and do the same thing at a theater.

Rayner could have brought him in that very day, but Sorin had asked him to watch the male. Learn about him. Figure out why it had taken them so long to catch up with him. Figure out what made him so godsdamn good at what he did. Rayner could admit he was looking forward to seeing the male's reaction to Sorin's proposition.

"I also know you are an excellent thief because you can read people," Sorin was saying. "You have learned to watch others and figure out what makes them tick. You know how to find weaknesses and exploit them. You know how to do this without the other person realizing they have been swindled until it is done and you are long gone. That is talent, my friend." He tipped his glass in salute at Cyrus before taking another drink.

"I know I'm good at what I do," Cyrus drawled, swiping up his cards and putting them in order. "If you dragged me all the way here to congratulate me on effectively robbing your subjects, you could have just asked me to come. You didn't need to send the Ash Rider after me."

"His name is Rayner," Sorin said conversationally, organizing his own hand. "Between him and his network of contacts, we have had eyes on you for a few years now."

"Fucking busybodies," Cyrus muttered, tossing some coin onto the table.

Sorin shrugged, placing his own bet in the middle of the table. "It is my job to protect my subjects' best interests. That includes learning who is robbing them blind."

Cyrus tossed his cards onto the table, pulling the coin towards himself. "Great. You solved the riddle. What are you going to do with me now?"

"Offer you a job."

"Fuck off," Cyrus snorted, picking up the glass and taking a long drink.

Sorin placed his forearms on the table, leaning in to Cyrus. "I meant what I said, Cyrus. You have a unique talent. One I could use in my Court."

"You want me to *work* for you?"

"Work *with* me."

"Semantics."

"I am having some…disagreements with the Earth Court regarding Artist fees. I want you to help me with negotiations. Use these skills of yours to help me figure out my best angles."

Cyrus's eyes narrowed. "Then what?"

Sorin sat back, raking the cards in and shuffling them. "If we work well together and get along like I suspect we will, I want you to be my Second."

Cyrus went completely still. "Come again?"

"I know it sounds out of the blue to you, but like I said, Rayner has been watching you for the last few years. He has been reporting back everything he has learned about you. There is a weakness in my Court, and I think you can help fix that."

"Why not make him your Second?"

Sorin glanced at Rayner, and the Ash Rider shrugged.

"Because he is my Third. He is also my personal spy and is often gone for long periods of time. I need my Second to be more accessible."

"You hardly know me," Cyrus said.

"Hence the trial run with the Earth Court, but I think I know enough from what Rayner has gathered. I trust his opinions," Sorin said, dealing the cards once more. "I already have rooms prepared for you if you accept."

"Live here?" Cyrus asked, picking up his cards.

"Rayner has another residence in the city, but he mostly stays here. You are free to do whatever you like, but you will always have rooms available here as well."

The male just stared back at Sorin as if the idea of a place to call his own was foreign to him.

"So let me get this straight: I help you negotiate with the earth prick, and if you get all warm and gooey inside over how well we work together, you want me to be your Second-in-Command. What's the catch?"

Sorin tossed some coin onto the table. "I have my eye on a new general for my forces. She is kind of difficult to get along with. You would have to deal with her."

Cyrus scoffed. "A female? That's the catch?"

Sorin and Rayner exchanged a look. Cyrus had no idea what exactly this *female* could do to him. Rayner was a rare Ash Rider and even he avoided Eliza when she was in a foul-mood.

"Fuck it," Cyrus finally said when he won the next round of cards again. "I'm in."

"Why?" Sorin asked curiously.

"Like you said," he answered, knocking back the rest of his drink with a smirk. "I'm excellent at reading people."

Sorin chuckled, glancing at Rayner again. "You in?"

Rayner nodded, grabbing the liquor bottle and bringing it to the table, sliding it over to Cyrus as Sorin dealt him in. He kept his eye on Cyrus while they played. It wasn't his official role anymore, but it was ingrained in him at this point to constantly be guarding his sovereign's back.

Only now that sovereign was more friend-turned-family than prince he served out of any sort of obligation. He'd sworn allegiance to him a year ago, the Mark on his chest proof of that vow. It had been hard to get used to, learning that he could depend on someone else. Trusting after doing so much on his own for so long.

He'd brought Aravis's body back with him that day six years ago. Sorin had performed her Farewell Rites himself. He'd been there waiting for her, just as Rayner had asked him to be in case he did not survive Moranna. Sorin and the Water Prince had stepped in, taking control of everything the moment Sorin had seen him step off the ship carrying Aravis's body wrapped tightly in his cloak. He'd been nothing, going through the motions to get innocent people somewhere safe. He'd never been more grateful to not be alone. To have someone there to take over when he had nothing left to give.

"Since you two assholes apparently know my life story, what's yours?" Cyrus asked, dealing the next hand.

Sorin paused, his glass halfway to his lips, shooting a glance at Rayner. He knew the prince would intervene if Rayner wanted him to, but Rayner just sent the thief a dark grin. "Do you know what a dreamer's lie is?" he asked, picking up his cards.

"Do tell," Cyrus murmured.

"That all nightmares have an end. Some never do. I didn't know if mine ever would," Rayner replied, tossing coin onto the table to place his bet.

"And now?" Cyrus asked, refilling his drink.

"Depends on the day," Rayner answered truthfully.

Cyrus snickered, toasting him with his glass. "I hear that."

And hours later, when the thief was passed out on one of the over-stuffed sofas and Rayner was still seated next to Sorin at the table, sipping on a final glass of liquor, he asked, "What do you think?"

Sorin knocked back the last of his drink, mulling over his thoughts. "He has his own darkness to overcome."

"We all do."

"Do you think he can do it?" Sorin asked, setting his glass down with a faint thud.

"I think he'll make an excellent Second if he can face his nightmares," Rayner answered. "They won't end until he does."

They sat in silence for a long moment before Sorin said, "He will fit in well. Balance us all out, especially once Eliza is ready to be part of this Inner Court when she is ready."

"You think she will accept?"

Sorin snickered. "A chance to take the position from a male and prove herself? She is as bloodthirsty as they come. You know that."

"And her nightmares?" Rayner pressed.

Sorin's grin fell, his features turning grave. "Together. If we can all learn to trust each other, to depend on each other, we can face those nightmares. If we can do that, we will be a force on this continent."

"It'll take time," Rayner supplied.

"We've got time," Sorin answered. "The war is settling. Our people are safe. We take the time to do this right to ensure they remain so."

"Whatever it takes then," Rayner said.

Sorin nodded. "Whatever it takes."

Leaving Cyrus to sleep off his alcohol in the den, they went up to the floor where their private rooms were located. But when Sorin went to his chambers, Rayner continued up to the top floor. It had been a long night, and the sun would be rising soon.

Fire Court Third.

Another name he now went by.

And as he watched the sun break over the horizon, he couldn't help but wonder what other names the Oracle had glimpsed in his future.

A NOTE FROM THE AUTHOR

Oh man! Keeping this novella a secret while I was writing it was SO HARD! Not even my alpha readers got sneak peeks until it was done (much to their dismay. Haha!) But I think it was worth the wait.

I knew there was no way I could ever fully tell Rayner's story within the *Darkness* books themselves, so when I first started to entertain some novella ideas, I immediately knew Rayner would have one. Our quiet, brutal, vengeful Ash Rider who has a soft spot for a little girl named Tula. One of the biggest questions I've gotten is why is Rayner so attached to her? I hope by understanding his past, you understand his actions a little more. And how about those throwbacks to the Inner Court before they were even a thing? Writing about Cyrus, Sorin, and Rayner when they were first getting to know each other was some much needed delight in the middle of the Rayner's tragic past because let me tell you, I was *sobbing* writing that last chapter when Aravis died!

But here we are, the end of another story that's leading up to the biggest finale of all. The final book in the *Lady of Darkness* series will release on March 30, 2023. It's available now for preorder on Amazon!

Until next time, Friends. Wishing you a day full of caffeine and dragons- Melissa

LET'S STAY CONNECTED!

My social links are below, but I'd also like to extend a special invitation to you to join my reader group on Facebook at Melissa's Nook & Posse. I drop teasers as I'm writing new books, share about my writing process, my life, and love interacting with all of you. I'd love it if you joined us.

To stay up-to-date on release dates, new series, and more, be sure and sign up for the newsletter, too!

WHERE TO FIND ME!

- Website: www.melissakroehrich.com
- Instagram: @melissa_k_roehrich
- TikTok: @authormelissakroehrich
- Facebook Page: Melissa K. Roehrich
- Facebook Reader Group: Melissa's Nook & Posse
- Pinterest: @melissa_k_roehrich

Made in the USA
Middletown, DE
05 September 2024